FACEOFF
NORTHBROOK HOCKEY ELITE

Rebecca Connolly
Heather B. Moore
Sophia Summers

FACEOFF
NORTHBROOK HOCKEY ELITE

Copyright © 2019 by Rebecca Connolly
Print edition
All rights reserved

No part of this book may be reproduced in any form whatsoever without prior written permission of the publisher, except in the case of brief passages embodied in critical reviews and articles. This is a work of fiction. The characters, names, incidents, places, and dialogue are products of the author's imagination and are not to be construed as real.

Interior design by Cora Johnson
Edited by Kelsey Down and Lorie Humpherys
Cover design by Rachael Anderson
Cover image credit: Deposit Photos #82835504
Published by Mirror Press, LLC

ISBN: 978-1-947152-82-3

NORTHBROOK HOCKEY ELITE SERIES

Faceoff
Powerplay
Rebound
Crosscheck
Breakaway
Shootout

Dedication

Thanks to Grizz for letting his younger brother have a story, and to Ryker for not getting in the way of my plans.

Shout out to the Chicago Blackhawks. Just because they're awesome. And because their games helped a girl whose only hockey experience was Miracle and Mighty Ducks to fall in love with an amazing sport.

Faceoff

She isn't supposed to want him. He isn't supposed to want her. But wanting each other is inevitable.

Clint McCarthy has finally achieved his dream of playing for a professional hockey program, and is eager to make his mark with his new team. While getting settled in his new city, he happens across Bree Stone, whom he has known for years, with their respective brothers both being in the famed Belltown Six Pack. But for the life of him, he can't remember Bree ever looking so attractive. Or being so captivating. Or taking over his every waking thought.

In the middle of her graduate degree, Bree has no time or desire for working on her dating life, or lack thereof, but the impossibly handsome Clint McCarthy coming back into her life makes everything complicated. She shouldn't be focusing on him, or on them, not when her professional future hangs in the balance. But once she hears about Clint's past with the Northbrook Hockey Elite program, and where that program stands now, Bree just might find a way to make her career, and a future with Clint, come to life.

ONE

"I don't know why you're dragging me into this."

"You love doing this, don't lie."

"Actually, I don't. It's not my type of scene."

"Not your scene? It's the guys, bro. You've known them since you were a kid."

"A teenager, thanks. You're not that much older than me, and they are *your* friends. Not mine."

"Don't tell any of them that. They specifically told me to bring you. Wouldn't want anyone to think it was personal."

Clint McCarthy rolled his eyes and bit back a sigh of resignation as he followed his older and, admittedly, larger brother into the restaurant. It wasn't often that Grizz pulled him into one of the semiannual Six Pack gatherings, but when he did, Clint was always left feeling out of place.

That sort of thing tended to happen when six of the most popular professional baseball players in the world got together. They'd all played on the same team in college at Belltown University and made a sort of history all getting drafted, then defied further odds by all getting called up to the majors. The news outlets were full of random reports and gossip about them, and the favorite segue on any channel was "Speaking of the Six Pack . . ."

Clint didn't mind having a famous older brother; most of the time he was pretty amused by the thing. He would be a wealth of information for any reporter wanting a more real and embarrassing side of Grizz McCarthy, not that he'd ever seriously consider doing such an expose.

Grizz would fight back with one of his own, and Clint was fairly certain there were just as many stories about him as there were about Grizz.

That wouldn't help him get called up at all.

"Heard anything from Marcus yet?" Grizz asked as the two of them pushed their way through the regular Friday night crowd at Corky's Brewhouse.

Clint shook his head at the mention of their agent, one of the rare kind that worked with athletes in two different sports—and it was even rarer that two of his clients were brothers. "Nope. I'm not expecting anything for at least one more year. Two seasons with the Rays isn't enough to make a point when I've been gone so long."

Grizz looked over his shoulder with the sort of scolding look only a brother could give. "You're a star, Clint. Anyone can see that. I've read the reports on you, and it's only a matter of time."

There was nothing to say to that, so Clint only shrugged. Grizz was as good a guy as ever walked the earth, but there was no changing the fact that he was always going to think Clint was better than the reality just because he was his brother. Besides, Grizz played baseball, not hockey.

His brother would have argued that he knew enough about any given sport to be a good judge anywhere, but Clint refused to accept that.

Taking four years away from the sport to serve in the

Marines had seemed the obvious choice to Clint at the time, and he would never regret a single moment he had spent on active duty, but there was no denying that it had affected his playing. Oh, he'd kept in prime physical shape—the Marines made sure of that—but being away from the game for that long...

No amount of solo drills on whatever ice he could find when free to do so could compensate for that loss.

Four years of active duty. Now he was starting his third reserve year, as well as his third season in minor league hockey, and he felt tugged in both directions.

He'd chosen the Marines when he hadn't been drafted, thanks to a season-altering knee injury in the middle of his senior year of high school. Two years of junior college to get back into prime shape, and when he still hadn't been picked up, he'd walked away. He'd served his country well, made good connections, and matured, which some might have argued was his most valuable development.

But his love and passion for hockey hadn't gone away.

The fact that Grizz's agent had called Clint and offered to represent him before his active duty years were up had shocked Clint, and the ball hadn't stopped rolling yet.

The Rays had taken a huge chance on him, despite not being one of the better minor league teams, and he would be forever grateful they had.

Someone might have pulled some strings to get him there, considering they were an affiliate for the team with the best coach in the nation, arguably. He had no grand ideas of being called up to play for the Hawks in St. Louis, but to play for Jon Singleton would be beyond his most insane dreams.

But none of that was on the table tonight. In the brief lull between when their season drew to a close and his season hadn't really begun, the Six Pack had decided to meet up in

Cincinnati before Cole Hunter's team started their World Series run. That, of course, meant at least one of them would be having a dry evening, and since Clint was starting his season and was always alcohol free in season, there would be two of them.

If any of the Six Pack's ladies were around, however . . .

Well, Clint didn't want to assume anything, but he wouldn't be surprised if one or two of them had some sort of announcement about certain additions, and then the whole evening could be a dry one.

None of them were especially excessive drinkers, but the degree of one's social drinking did tend to fluctuate depending on who was around. And there was no telling what anyone in the Six Pack would do at any given time. Then there was the possibility of any in-season bets that had yet to be paid . . .

Sudden images of his brother in a chicken suit flashed into Clint's mind, and he grinned with all the mischievous deviousness any little brother in the world ever possessed.

"What's that for?" Grizz asked in alarm, catching a glimpse of his expression before Clint could clear it.

Clint shrugged again. "Just a funny thought. Never mind. Hey, is everyone coming?"

"Think so," Grizz grunted. "The guys, anyway. Rach couldn't get away, Harlow's coming in late tonight, Erica drove down, but the rest . . . "

Clint's head spun with the names. Rachel he knew well, as she was his brother's wife, but he barely kept up with the rest. In the last few years, there had been three weddings, and he'd gone to them all, but as to who had yet to tie the knot . . .

"Grizz and company in the house!" someone bellowed as they entered the private room that had been reserved for them at Corky's, and Grizz, ever the enthusiastic socialite, raised both arms into the air with a whoop better suited for an arena than a dining room.

What a goon.

Clint slowly shook his head and slid his hands into the pockets of his brown leather jacket, worn to just the right texture in just the right places. Now the entertainment would, allegedly, begin.

And the inquisition.

"Hi there," a stunning woman completely out of the league of any man in the room greeted him as she came over to Clint with a dazzling smile.

Swallowing the lump in his throat associated with the confrontation of such glamorous beauty, Clint straightened as much as he was able, though he was already six foot three and nearly as big as his brother. "Hi."

The beauty's smile widened. "You don't remember me. That's surprisingly charming." She held out a hand. "Trista."

Idiocy, that fabulous friend, smacked Clint upside the head, and he found himself smiling sheepishly. "Right. Right, I'm sorry. Clint McCarthy." He shook her hand and was impressed by the strength in her grip.

"I could tell," Trista said with a laugh, tilting her head towards Grizz, now thumping a few of the guys on their backs. "You and Grizz are practically twins."

Clint grinned knowingly. "The McCarthy curse, I'm afraid. The four of us boys could each pass for any of the others. Grizz has the best beard, though. Or so he tells us all. I still think my scruff is better." He leaned closer to whisper, "And I'm faster than he will ever be."

Trista tossed her head back and laughed. "Does he know that?"

"Everybody knows that, babe," Ryker Stone assured her as he came up beside Trista, slipping an arm around her waist possessively while brushing a light kiss on her cheek. "Hey, Clint."

"Rabbit." Clint shook Ryker's hand firmly, smirking as he used the guy's nickname, as they all did. It was second nature to do so, given the closeness of the Six Pack and the brotherhood they shared, and being a Six Pack sibling, Clint was included in that.

Sort of.

"Good season this year?" Ryker asked, tucking his free hand into the pocket of his dark fitted jeans.

"Could be. Got some fresh blood after a few trades." There wasn't anything to do but shrug yet again. The team was still learning their rhythm, and Clint's line, while the fastest, was also the one with the most misses.

Communication seemed to be a problem with them, and it could hold all of them back from moving up if they didn't figure it out soon.

"Season?"

Clint smiled at Trista's perplexed question. "Hockey."

"Clint plays center for ... " Ryker looked at him with wide eyes, confusion swirling. "The Rays?"

"Very good," Clint confirmed with a nod. "Starting my third season with them."

Trista held up a hand in defense or surrender. "I know absolutely nothing about hockey, Clint, and I admit that freely."

"Well, as long as you admit it, that's fine," he teased, nodding when his brother silently inquired if he wanted a drink from across the room. "I'm the guy in the middle waiting for the puck to drop."

"Basically, Clint plays Hungry Hungry Hippos with one puck and a stick." Ryker raised a brow, daring Clint to argue the point.

He wasn't going to; Ryker was one of the nicest guys on the planet, and Clint couldn't exactly say he was wrong. A bit simplistic, slightly inaccurate, but the concept fit.

It was a stretch, but he'd let it slide.

"And where are you?" Trista asked him, nodding at the explanation from Ryker, evidently tucking it away for future reference. "I mean, where does your team play?"

"Clint!" Cole Hunter bellowed, coming up behind Clint and thumping him hard. "My, my, how you've grown! Almost as big as Grizz now."

Clint rolled his eyes. "Thanks, Big Dawg." He gave Ryker and Trista a despairing look. "This is what I get for beating the Dallas minor league team last week. It's not my fault Dawg places bets on the wrong squad."

Ryker shook his head, smiling. "The Rays are the affiliate of the Hawks, aren't they?"

"Sure are!" Grizz handed a glass of soda to Clint, nodding with pride. "Lansing is fine and all, but we've gotta get Clint down to St. Louis. Fans are incredible in that city; I hate when we have to play. Great teams, for sure, but those fans . . . " He whistled and shuddered. "Being the visiting team is brutal. Dylan Proctor is starting third right now out there, and he says he'll never leave."

Sawyer Bennett joined them now, his grin eerily identical to his sister, Rachel, Grizz's wife. "Dylan Proctor happens to be in a position to actually dictate where he plays and for how long. Not everybody else has that freedom."

And just like that, the conversation switched from hockey to baseball, which tended to happen in settings like this. Clint had never met Dylan Proctor or any of the other players they were mentioning that had played for St. Louis, so he had nothing to add to the conversation as he stood there like a sidekick in an old-school superhero film.

He wasn't sure whom he was sidekick *to* in this scenario, but it was entirely possible that the entire Six Pack, as a whole, was the superhero.

They did have something supernatural about them, come to think of it.

"Hey, kid."

Clint turned in surprise to see Levi Cox, otherwise known as Steal, lingering at the edge of the group, smiling only slightly.

That was pretty much the only way Levi smiled.

"Steal. How are you, man?"

Levi shook his hand hard. "Can't complain. Heard you go by Fido now. Trying to compete with Big Dawg?"

Clint laughed once. "Not even a little. And how'd you hear about that?"

"Pete Crawley went to high school with me, and we had a reunion a month ago." Levi exhaled, his broad shoulders slowly relaxing as he did so. "What are your chances of getting called up, huh?"

Normally, Clint hated this question. It was impossible to say, and it really wasn't anybody's business if he played minor or major, considering he was fortunate to be playing hockey at all. But Levi was different; he understood the battle and the drive, wouldn't judge a player of any sport for the level at which he played, and respected the process.

Mostly.

"I don't know," Clint admitted, nodding as the final member of the Six Pack, Axel Diaz, came up to them silently. "My first season with the Rays was tough, second fantastic, and this year will probably be somewhere in the middle."

"Come on," Axel protested, shaking his arm in protest. "You're lightning, man! I went to a game last season, remember?"

Clint gave him a dubious look. "That was a good night. No one gets called up for one good night."

Levi hadn't reacted, only listened. "What does your agent say?"

"Same as always. Getting there, hearing chatter, stick with it . . . " Clint smiled at the pair of them without humor. "Noncommittal to the full. I'm just fortunate to be playing, and I know it."

"Don't sell yourself short, kid," Levi grunted with a very brotherly look. "You've earned this."

Clint grinned at Levi, then at Axel as he thumped him on the back in encouragement. "Can I take you guys back to Lansing to be my roommates or something? This is great for my ego."

They laughed and pretended to debate the idea, though he knew they were all mostly settled where they were now. Well, as settled as a professional athlete ever is. There's always a risk of trade, and each of them had learned over the years that you go where your team is.

And your team can change in an instant.

Slowly, Clint sipped his soda, trying to remember the last real team he had played on. Not counting the Marines, of course, which was far more of a brotherhood than a team. But a real, honest-to-goodness hockey team. One where your line is practically three parts of the same heartbeat, where your defense is a reflex of the offense, and the goalie calls out things a millisecond before you can anticipate it.

Such a team was a rarity. A good hockey player could play for almost any team, with almost any collection of equally talented guys, and make a run of it. But that feeling of team, that unity and clarity . . .

That had only happened once in Clint's life, and it had been ages ago.

A buzzing in his back pocket broke him from his reminiscence of teenage kids on the ice rinks of Chicago, and he pulled his phone free to glance at the screen.

Frowning, he excused himself from Levi and Axel and moved closer to a window, one hand covering his free ear as he held the phone up.

"Marcus? I can barely hear you."

"This'll only take a second, buddy. Are you sitting down?"

Clint snorted softly. "Are you kidding? I'm with the Six Pack."

There was a laugh from the other end of the line that seemed too entertained by that. "That's perfect. Absolutely perfect, I couldn't have scripted this better. Tell Grizz to return my calls."

"Marcus . . ."

"You settled in Lansing?"

Clint heaved a sigh and shifted his weight with some reluctance. "It's been two years; I should hope so."

"Time to unsettle. This is your call, my friend."

Something tight suddenly clenched the center of Clint's chest, and his vision seemed to freeze and cloud over without actually losing any clarity.

"My . . . my what?"

Marcus cackled almost maniacally from his end of the call. "I told you we could get you there, Clint! You're in St. Louis next week, you join the Hawks while early in the season, and we have got you up with the big dogs, man! I'm emailing you details right now, so you finish up the Six Pack party and get ready for your own stardom!"

There were other things his agent said—Clint could hear him saying them—but the words themselves were lost on him.

This was his call.

FACEOFF

He was going to the pros. He was joining the Hawks. Everything he had ever wanted for his professional life was happening now.

Right now.

He lowered his phone, thumb automatically ending the call, quite possibly hanging up on his insane agent. Eyes wide, he turned around, automatically preparing to search for his brother among the rest.

He didn't have to look hard.

Every eye in the room was on him, and there was no other conversation.

Grizz's eyes seemed as round as his own felt, and through his brother's ever-impressive beard, a mouth formed the word, "Well?"

Clint could only swallow. "I just got called up."

For the space of exactly one and a half heartbeats, nothing happened.

Then there was an explosion of sound, emotion, and feeling as the entire Six Pack rushed in on him, whooping and hollering as though they'd just won some national championship thanks to Clint. Grizz outdid them all by throwing his arms around Clint and actually heaving him off of the ground as he chanted something unintelligible, crushing Clint's ribs with every syllable. Hands thumped and slapped Clint's arms, shoulders, and back, before the entire mob of them started jumping up and down in the traditional way every team seemed to in celebration of something huge.

An earsplitting whistle rent the air, and, delirious with twenty thousand emotions, Clint turned to face the sound with the rest.

Cole Hunter stood there on a table, of course, a full glass extended out in one hand. "A toast, men!"

They all scrambled for the nearest drink, full or not, and raised their glasses in the air.

"To Baby Brother McCarthy," Cole intoned with mock solemnity. "May he rank higher than Grizz ever did in *Sports Monthly*'s Hottie Issue, but not as high as me."

Someone whistled while Clint's hair was ruffled as if he were nine years old.

"And to the Hawks for getting the best friggin' center the ice has ever seen!"

Cheers went up again.

"And!" Cole hollered over the sound. "And to us. All of us. For getting our butts on my jet to watch Fido freaking McCarthy play his very first home game in the great city of St. Louis!"

Thunder couldn't have sounded louder than their cheers and celebrations on that note, and Clint, barely conscious of anything but elation and exhilaration, faintly reminded himself to call his mother when all this was over.

Provided Grizz didn't beat him to it.

TWO

THE PROCESS BY which interest rates accrued had to be the most boring subject on the entire planet.

Or, at least, Dr. Glass made it seem that way. His voice just droned on and on and on . . .

She had been a finance minor in her undergraduate years, but Bree Stone could not, for the life of her, see why anyone would take more courses than absolutely necessary from this instructor. He seemed as bored by the subject material as she was.

Glancing around the room, she amended her statement: as bored as the entire class was.

Three of them in the back were asleep, and the only reason Dr. Glass hadn't done something about it was because the fool had turned the lights down for his presentation. There were maybe twenty people in the class, and he treated it like a massive undergraduate lecture.

Amateur mistake for the dinosaur professor.

Bree checked her phone quickly before sliding it back to its usual place in her back pocket, sighing with relief that there were only two minutes left in this lecture.

And this was a graduate-level class? Lectures weren't supposed to be given anymore. Not in the same way, and not at this level of tedium. All of her other classes up to this point, third semester in, had been fairly hands-on and more of a discussion. Some with PowerPoint presentations, sure, but there was a certain level of engagement with these graduate students, who had already proven themselves competent adults, if not professionals, in the topic of discussion.

If only they would be treated as such.

"That is all for today," Dr. Glass intoned without any level of inflection different from his entire lecture. For the inattentive, his words would have been completely lost, and they might continue sleeping right into the next class, which, if she recalled correctly, was Accounting 101.

Brutal for those who couldn't tolerate revisiting basics.

Whistling under her breath, Bree slid her hardly touched notebook into her bag and headed for the door of the classroom.

As if her schedule dictated her social contact, her phone vibrated the moment she passed through the doors.

One glance told her all she needed to know, and she raised the phone to her ear.

"Hello, brother mine," she said in a flat tone that belied the smile on her face.

"Sister dear."

"It's a bit creepy to get a call the moment I step out of class. It's like you know my schedule."

"I do know your schedule. I have to know when my best chance of reaching you might be."

Bree snorted softly, adjusting the strap of her bag on her shoulder. "I'm not in class constantly. I haven't started any internships yet..."

"What are you going to do for that, by the way?" Ryker

interrupted without missing a beat. "It's about time to get that set, isn't it? Your final semester?"

"Okay, now I am definitely creeped out. I know we've never talked about my educational timelines, deadlines, or any other kind of lines." She glanced over her shoulder as she left the building, only seeing other students before returning to the campus and overcast skies ahead of her. "You're not following me, are you? Lying about your fabulous baseball career and really just following me around for a living?"

Ryker's laugh was as warm and familiar as home. "I can't see how that would be profitable, and Trista might object to my being a stalker for a living. And I have an alibi presently. I'm sitting in my hotel room with Benj Miller. He says hi."

Bree laughed and lifted her fingers in a half wave to an acquaintance she passed on campus. "Well, hello, Benj Miller. I bet he looks hot in Houston. That is where you are, isn't it?"

"First of all, no. Second of all, Bree, yes, we are in Houston for the kids camp and charity game. Seriously, Bree?"

"Ryker, I'm twenty-two and red-blooded, and I have twenty-twenty vision. Benj Miller is gorgeous, and if Trista hasn't told you that by now, then your wife's eyesight is horrible."

Her brother groaned from the other end of the line. "No, Bree. He's my teammate and a puppy, and it would be all kinds of wrong. And he can hear me saying this right now! Just no. *No*, Benj. Shut up. Teammate rule. Have boundaries. No. Moving on." He cleared his throat awkwardly. "How's life?"

Bree sighed with a smile and turned to sit on a bench near a tree whose leaves were just beginning to turn for the fall. "Life. Life is going on."

Ryker gave a very unsatisfying grunt at that. "That's not a great answer."

"Grad school is not a great experience," she admitted.

"I'm enjoying it, don't get me wrong, but it's kinda like conditioning. Hate every minute, but you know it's good for you, so a part of you enjoys it?"

"Okay . . . with you so far."

Bree wrinkled up her nose. "I do like what I'm doing, or I think I will once I'm out of here, but it's just . . . school . . . "

"Fair enough. You seeing anyone?"

"Benj Miller."

She could hear Ryker coughing over the line, and she grinned at the sound. "Very funny," Ryker remarked dryly. "I might be sick at the suggestion."

"For my part or for his?"

"Are you really seeing anyone?"

"Of course not." Bree scoffed and leaned back against the bench, stretching her legs out. "You know me, nobody's interested and I'm not that social."

"Hey now," her brother scolded in an entirely brotherly manner. "There is no *of course* in this situation, Bree. You are a beautiful young woman, smarter than anyone your age should be and funnier than any of my teammates. Clearly something is wrong with that school you're at, or at least the men on that campus."

Bree hummed a laugh. "Right, should I go around putting up signs that say *Ryker Stone cordially invites you to date his sister*? That'll start a great line of your fanboys, or the ones in love with my sister-in-law, but how does that help me?"

"Come on . . . "

"Why do I have to have a romantic life anyway? What's that got to do with anything?" She folded her arms, shaking her head even though her brother wouldn't be able to see or hear it. "I have a business degree and a finance minor to my name, and a master of public administration coming. Once school is done, I'll be way too busy to worry about a guy, of all things."

There was silence on the other end of the line, then Ryker laughed, and laughed hard.

"It's not funny!" Bree insisted, though she was laughing too.

"No, it's not, but I'm just so proud of you. You're just going to tackle the world, aren't you? You don't need me looking after you or worrying about you. You're too strong. Heaven help anybody, man or woman, who gets in your way."

Bree looked at her phone in amusement, then replaced it at her ear. "You okay, Ryker? That sounded like a signing-off speech. You're not going to resign from your position as overprotective brother now just because I talk a big game, are you?"

"I'll never resign, sis. I'm Team Bree for life."

"Sorry not sorry. Good luck tonight. If my roommates aren't hogging the TV, I'll be watching. Thanks for the link, by the way. Livestream is great."

"No worries. Season's over, and Cole's jet works great if you want to come out any time. Hey, quick question. Do you like hockey?"

Bree smirked to herself. "That's the one on the ice, right?"

"Correct. Good memory."

"It's all right. Not a huge fan, but I can't say my exposure's all that great. I've got a brother who plays baseball, so that pretty much ruled all our lives."

"Ha ha. Well, Grizz's brother Clint got called up, so he'll be coming out there. We all want to come to a game, so I thought it would be great to have you come along, since you're out there too."

Bree sobered and sat up, her smirk turning into a smile.

"Yeah, that'd be great! Clint's going to be out here? Another Six Pack Sib in the vicinity?"

"You guys have a name?"

"It's a support group. Very serious, and we have matching pins and everything. Now I won't have to Skype into the monthly meetings alone. That's fantastic."

"I'm hanging up now. Love you, kid."

"Love you, too, weirdo. Bye, Benj!"

There was a loud call in response from the background, but Ryker ended the call before she could make it out.

Still, she was laughing pretty hard about it.

Her brother was a nut. Nice, but a nut. Even with his insane professional baseball schedule, he called her every week, sometimes multiple times. He hadn't done that during her undergraduate years, but she'd only lived forty minutes from home then. Her parents had her home every weekend, and she'd grown almost sick of Baltimore over those four years.

No one had quite expected her to head out to the Midwest for graduate school, let alone all the way out to St. Louis. There was no family out here, no old friends, and nothing but the program she would devote herself to.

And she loved it. Absolutely loved it. Aside from the class she had just escaped from, that is.

Being in a program that wasn't directly related to mathematics proved to help a lot when it came to family intervention, as did the distance. Her father was a professor of math, and a nerd in the field in his own right. Her mother wasn't a mathematician, but she had started a non-profit and volunteered in the community, and she loved nothing more than being involved with her kids.

No math; not local.

She spoke with her parents every Sunday, and her mom

called randomly during the week, usually during class. Sometimes Bree called her back.

Sometimes she "forgot."

The only one in her family to really give her a respectful distance was Trista, her sister-in-law. That might be because Trista was a movie star. Oscar nominated, even, and currently starring in one of the most popular television shows on the air. Trista was just as obsessed with math as Bree's dad was, which would have bewildered anyone who knew, and she had gone back to school to get a master's in the subject.

Bree loved math herself, just not enough to devote her life to it. Yes, she still recited the numerals of pi when she needed to calm herself, and her doodles in her notebook might be algebraic equations at times, but she was a mix of both her parents, it seemed.

Nonprofits intrigued her, but so did public management, and her business degree could only help her there.

But what did she want to do?

No idea.

Ryker had learned not to ask that question, as she had given him so many sarcastic answers over the years. Complete deflection from actually considering it.

Everyone thought she had it all together. *Bree knows exactly what she's doing. Bree's got a plan. Bree's so organized.*

Bree was almost clueless.

Nobody knew that, of course, but that was the thing about being in school; reality was delayed while you were in it.

She didn't have to know yet.

Did she?

Making a face, Bree opened her email and found, to her complete lack of surprise, a message from her advisor.

Only a few weeks to submit your request for internship. If you need reminding of the guidelines, let me know.

Bree closed her email quickly and shoved her phone away.

She didn't need reminding; she knew exactly what the requirements were. They danced around her head when she was trying to sleep at night.

That was the reality of life trying to sneak its way into her university life.

Not cool.

Rising from the bench, she shouldered her bag and made her way through campus, her apartment being on the exact opposite side from where her final class of the day had been. She'd opted to live with other girls in the same graduate school, though their programs were different. They'd met at a social over the summer during an introduction weekend, and since Bree had no local friends to speak of and no desire to pay the exorbitant price of quality off-campus housing alone, she'd agreed.

Amy and Penny were great, for an almost-blind pairing of roommates. They weren't crazy social, which suited Bree perfectly, but they were just social enough to give her some decent alone time in the apartment, which was even more perfect. Every now and then, they invited her along. Sometimes she agreed. Other times they all sat home together in sweats and watched a movie.

That was her favorite kind of night.

Bree's more social nights hadn't exactly gone according to plan.

A telltale buzzing made Bree sigh, and she turned her bag to fumble within it for her phone. Her thumb was already sliding to the ignore button as she pulled the phone out to glance at the screen, but she paused when she saw who was calling.

Hesitation ran a course along her arms, and she pursed her lips as the ringing continued.

Sighing, she answered and put the phone to her ear. "Hi, Trista."

"Hey, you!"

There was just something about the perky edge to Trista's voice that made Bree both smile and cringe, but that was her sister-in-law to a T. Trista was bright like sunshine, which could be overwhelming, but she also held the same warmth as sunshine, and Bree heard that too.

"How's the shoot?" Bree asked as she continued on the path towards home.

She could almost hear Trista shrug. "Eh. It's a filler episode, and my character isn't a major player in it."

"Spoiler alert!" Bree covered her free ear with a dramatic flair that wouldn't be seen.

"You don't watch the show. You know it, and I know it."

Bree's smile spread. "The trailers are always good."

"I'll tell the team." There was a beat, and then Trista gingerly asked, "How did the other night go?"

She was the only one who could ask Bree that question; she was the only one who even knew about the other night.

She was also the only one Bree would actually give an answer to that question.

"Remember Paxton from high school?" Bree muttered, lowering her voice despite having no one close enough to overhear.

"No . . . " Trista moaned. "I mean, yes, I do, but no . . . Sweetie . . . "

Bree shook her head quickly. "It's fine. It's fine! Just the same thing. The guy just wanted more than I was willing to give. Again."

"He's done that before?"

"No!" Bree looked around, realizing belatedly how loud her answer had been. "Oh my gosh, Trista. It's just what always happens. I've only gone out with him once. I only go out with any of them once."

"That can't be true."

"I promise you it is." She craned her neck and sighed heavily, something she would never have done on this particular topic with her brother. "I know there are good guys in the area; I've met them. They're all married or serious enough to be. So why do I only attract the ones that look nice but are just a waste of time?"

"Welcome to the question of most of the actresses I know, babe."

Bree rolled her eyes as she crossed the street to her complex. "Great. Living up the Hollywood life over here in St. Louis. I don't even know why I bother."

"I'm sorry, Bree. It's just not fair."

"I wasn't aware that dating was in the court of fair play," Bree mused. "More of a kill-or-be-killed game, isn't it?"

Trista snorted a soft laugh. "Careful, Bree. Your inner cynic is showing."

"I might just let her roam free for a while. Forget about dating and guys and whatever else, and just focus on school. I need to find an internship for next semester, and that might not be local anyway. A relationship now would just get in the way."

"Hmm. Convincing me or yourself?"

Reaching for the keys in the front pocket of her backpack, Bree coughed a humorless laugh. "Stating. Emphatically. Not doing it, officially."

"Okay. I'll put an ad in the paper."

"Nobody reads the paper anymore, Trista. Are you looking over a script for a period piece or something?"

"I might be. You home now?"

Bree pushed open the front door, which emitted a loud squeal of emphasis. "Just walked in."

"'Kay. Let me know when you have a long weekend. We need a spa retreat. You're letting your hair go, and I miss the highlights and lowlights."

"I don't miss the maintenance of the color," Bree retorted as she dropped her bag on the floor and waved at Penny, who sat on the couch with a pint of ice cream and a textbook. "But I'll take the retreat."

"Love you, sis."

Bree paused in her just-got-home routine for a fond smile. "Love you too, Tris. Bye."

Setting the phone down on the kitchen table, Bree sank into the nearest chair with a heavy exhale.

"That sounded serious," Penny announced. "Care to share?"

Bree waved a tired hand. "Just swearing off dating and men. Tired of the trouble."

Penny raised her pint in solidarity. "Preach, girl. There's another pint in the freezer. Grab it and dig in. I've got five more pages, and then I'm putting on a movie. You game?"

After the conversations she'd just had, that sounded amazing.

"I'm in," she replied, moving to the freezer. "Except my brother's got a charity game later, and I really should watch. I mean, he sent me the livestream link specifically so I could watch him."

"Fine by me." Penny grinned widely. "I've got a thing for Benj Miller. Hook a sister up?"

Bree laughed in surprise before heading over to the couch. "Actually, I might have an in there . . ."

THREE

"Get off the boards! Get off the boards!"

Clint struggled hard against the monster of a teammate currently smothering him into the plexiglass, panting harder than he should have been with the exertion of it. But Moose wasn't budging, so Clint did the only thing he could. Peeking in the only direction he could towards an open member of his current squad, he kicked the puck in his direction, which was instantly scooped up and sent in the direction of the goal.

Moose grunted and shoved off of Clint to go thundering towards the play while Clint struggled to find his lungs, currently caught between three or four ribs. But he couldn't show that, couldn't reveal any sign of weakness.

Two weeks with his team, and he was dying.

"Nice save, Fido!" someone called from the bench.

Clint wasn't sure if that was sincere or sarcastic, and he wasn't sure he cared. He raced as fast as he was able to help his team get the puck in the goal when the puck was suddenly cleared right at him.

He blinked for a millisecond, then scooped it up, weaving

his way towards the net, a new energy screaming its way down his legs. He called out without words, his teammates somehow comprehending his intentions by keeping the defense as occupied as possible.

"Hup!" his own defenders called from the line. "Hup! Hup!"

Time seemed to slow, and Clint could hear himself exhale slowly, the goal and its keeper looming before him.

His eyes flicked left and right, noting the location of defenders, then he jerked to his left, sliding the puck neatly between the legs of one player before delivering the most perfect slapshot of his life beneath the arm of the goalie.

The bench chanted their approval, and Clint was suddenly swarmed by his fellow teammates, all batting his helmet like they were his older brothers.

"Attaboy, Fido, atta kid!" Hook, their top right-sided defender and captain of the team, praised, thumping him hard on the back. "And after Moose flattened you? That's no small thing, bro. He was gunning for you all day."

"I noticed," Clint replied, forcing a combination of grin and grimace. "Did I steal his locker or something?"

Hook snorted once. "Nah. Moose was just really close with Jerky, and his arrest really shook Moose up."

"That's not my fault, is it?" Clint exhaled roughly as they skated their way to the bench while the next group lined up. "I already know I'm Jerky's replacement and him being gone is the only reason I'm here. I don't need the whole team taking it out on me."

"Knock it off, man," Hook all but ordered. "We all have our crap in this game. Petey got called up when Grayson Boes blew out his knee. Hotch rode the bench forever until an entire line got suspended. This isn't a temp position you just fill in for, all right? Just play the game."

FACEOFF

Another bat on his helmet, and Hook climbed over the boards into the bench, catching a tossed bottle of water easily. Clint followed him, sitting on the bench in silence.

The last two weeks had been an endless blur of practice and stress, trying to figure out team dynamics and keeping his head above the water. Some of the guys were great; others didn't care if he were there or not.

Clint wasn't sure he cared all that much either. He just wanted to play. His first game was next week, and until then, he didn't think he'd feel much like a member of the team.

It sounded stupid when he thought about it. He wasn't normally so sensitive to this sort of thing, or to anything, really. He usually just went with the flow and figured things out as he went.

This was different.

He didn't expect best friends—that sort of thing took time—but with the Rays he'd had a squad, and back with Northbrook, he'd had a bond.

This felt like just a cluster of guys on the ice.

It wasn't as easy to play under these conditions.

It was fine, but it wasn't easy.

"Nice shot, Fido," another teammate said, sitting down beside Clint. "We'll watch that one on replay a lot, huh?" He chuckled and downed some water. "And earlier, back during shootouts, that was wicked deke you had going on."

Clint turned to him, amused by the defender, who went by Cal on the ice, for reasons he didn't yet understand. "It went off the bar, Cal. Not that wicked."

Cal scoffed loudly, shaking his head. "Doesn't matter. You wigged Geezer out of his mind. That was a close call for him, and he knows it."

"Thanks, man." Clint had to smile as he watched the other guys play. Cal was just one of those guys that were never ruffled by anything and were always smiling. The guy would even smile doing line drills on the ice while the rest of the team was red-faced and close to vomiting.

Literally—that had been two days ago, and Cal had just smiled like he was having the time of his life.

Unnatural.

Coach Singleton's whistle sounded after another goal, and everybody left the bench and moved to center ice, joining the other players.

"Not a bad day, boys," Coach said, somehow managing to chomp on his gum and speak coherently at the same time, as usual. He was a former navy man and was now a bit stockier, but no less impressive. "We look quick, we look sleek, and Fido here's flying up the ice like he was born on it."

The unexpected praise caught Clint off guard, and he ducked his head slightly as his teammates rumbled their approval, tapping their sticks on the ice.

"We got the Hounds next week," Coach continued, looking around at each of them. "Forget about what happened last year, forget about anything in the past. I only want you focusing on this year and this game. This season. Everybody's gotta get a session in with Eric before Tuesday, and anybody feeling the slightest aches and pains, see Doc or Brad. No sense gutting it out needlessly game one. Get healthy, get strong, get your heads right. All clear?"

"Yes, Coach," the team answered as one.

Coach nodded and whistled, gesturing in a circle. "Five laps and hit the showers. Weights tomorrow, no ice. Get a good run in. That's all."

The team tapped their sticks on the ice repeatedly in unison in a sort of applause before Hook rose from the ice and tossed his helmet down. "Five laps, boys. Let's hit it."

Other helmets joined his on the ice as Clint and the

others followed suit, filing in line as they began their laps. Some players hated the laps or line drills at the end of an already-tough practice, but Clint liked this part. It got them back to the very basics of their sport.

Skating had always been relaxing to him. The sound of his blades slashing against the ice, a crisp, clean noise in chorus as all twenty of them glided along the rink. It took him back to being a kid on the ice on his grandfather's farm, or the early days on the community center ice when all the other kids were giggling and falling down and he was simply skating laps or weaving down center ice between imaginary players.

He felt most at peace in this space. The soundtrack of the ice was his favorite, and he'd have done twenty laps to keep it going.

"Fido," Cal suddenly said, coming up to skate alongside him. "You have plans tomorrow?"

Clint smirked at his teammate. "Other than kicking your trash at weights?"

"Nice try."

"Oh, planning an upset this time?"

"I'm taking that as a no." Cal raised a thick brow. "Belltown's playing at MSSL this weekend. You like college basketball?"

Clint reared back a little. "Yeah, I do, better than the pros. I didn't go to Belltown, though. That was Grizz."

"Same difference," Cal replied with a shake of his sweat-dampened hair. "You in?"

There was something hilarious about him and Grizz being referred to as "same difference." It was remarkably accurate. They looked more alike than the other McCarthy brothers, though there was no mistaking the relation between any of them, and they were the two that had gone most into athletics. Their personalities were similar, though Grizz was more social, and those similarities had led to the brothers being either the best of friends or the worst of enemies growing up.

Clint was sure his mom had feared for their lives at the hands of each other at least a dozen times in their youth.

"Sure," Clint replied as they started their fourth lap. "Why not? Who all's going?"

"So far, just you and me," Cal shot back, grinning in his usual way. "Hotch might be game; he's a baller in his spare time. Mario, Junior, and Fig are usually up for stuff. Sound like a good crew?"

Cal had listed off some of Clint's favorites on the team and none of the ones that seemed to have issues with him, so there was no hesitation.

"Absolutely."

● ● ● ● ●

Spending more than her usual amount of time with her roommates led Bree to do things that she couldn't normally be coerced to do.

Like attend a basketball game.

She liked most sports in general, probably more out of repeated exposure in her life than anything else, but she had also learned that without someone to cheer for, she never got that invested in it.

But it was Belltown playing her school, and while she didn't particularly care about the athletic programs at Missouri State at St. Louis, she had enough ties to both schools to make an appearance. That, and she'd heard great things about the churros at the basketball games here.

The arena was packed, which was no surprise, as there wasn't anything else going on in early November on campus, and MSSL was supposed to be pretty good this year. Everybody was decked out in yellow and blue, enough to make her eyes hurt with it. Or maybe that was just the bright-yellow color of the seats in the arena, the walls of the arena, and the shirts of the student section in the arena.

"I feel like I've been swallowed by Big Bird," Bree muttered to no one in particular as she, Penny, and Amy made their way to their seats.

"Oh, stop that," Amy teased, glancing over her shoulder with a smile. "You're standing out, wearing that shirt in here. I don't even think Belltown has a fan section here."

Bree glanced around quickly, knowing better, then tapped Amy's shoulder. "Sure they do." She pointed to the seats near the rafters in the northeast corner. "Right there."

Three rows of red and blue broke up the sea of yellow, but it wasn't much. Oh, every now and then there was a brave individual wearing red, but for the most part, only the passionate MSSL fans were here.

Poor Belltown.

"And down they go," Bree murmured, the words for her alone. She hadn't attended Belltown for undergrad, much to Ryker's dismay, but she still had fond ties to the school. Some of her greatest memories had been the trips to Massachusetts for her brother's games or events there. So many people that had been part of her life in childhood. Her teenage years, for the most part, Ryker had been in the pros, but the Six Pack never let the relationships fade.

She could still text the group of them and get a mass collection of responses from them, each one better than the last.

Her birthday texts were unfailingly epic.

Instead of having just one older brother, she really had six.

Which could be a bit annoying at times, but mostly it was great.

Mostly.

"Thank you for not wearing red," Penny called up to her as they continued lower into the bowels of the arena. "White is passable, and you won't stand out as much."

"You're welcome?" Bree shrugged with a bemused smile.

The truth of the matter was that Bree didn't own anything in MSSL colors, and she didn't particularly care to. There might be a gray T-shirt from the early days of her program tucked away in a dresser drawer, but that was about it.

Belltown shirts, on the other hand, could practically have a drawer of their own.

Ryker liked to distribute his alumni and athletic-booster swag among the family.

He was generous like that.

The three girls slid their way into their row towards their seats, earning glowers and grumbles from the fans around them, just as the tip-off occurred.

Bree watched without much interest as the teams darted back and forth on the court, the ball flying between and being dribbled around players with an almost-dizzying frequency. One didn't have to know basketball well to know these two teams were very skilled, and the MSSL fans wasted no time in letting Belltown know how they felt about opposition in their arena.

She eyed the Belltown team bench, no longer familiar with the names of any Belltown athletes, as she once might have been. But she knew the focused, almost-anxious looks those players wore, and the determined set of the coach's jaw. The players' mouths moved as they spoke to their teammates on the court, though none of the words were audible to anyone except those who sat just behind the bench.

MSSL scored the first points, earning a thundering marching sound from the student section, accompanied by a fitting anthem by the pep band. That was to be expected, she supposed, when their mascot was the Militiamen. The face of the mascot himself, decked out in a fitting historic uniform, wasted no time in hyping up the student section, his musket raised aloft.

"Ohhhhhhh, and where'd they go?" the student section chanted, mocking Belltown's usual Lumberjack cry with their own twist.

Bree's lips pursed, and air hissed out as she considered how that would have infuriated Ryker and any other proud Lumberjack.

Good thing she wasn't one.

Still, it did make her face tighten a bit.

Very strange.

The game continued on for a few minutes, Belltown scoring in return and MSSL answering those points, and so on. No great plays, no exceptional moments, just clean, talented basketball.

Time for food.

"I need a churro," Bree informed her roommates, gesturing up to the concourse. "You guys need anything?"

Amy handed her a five-dollar bill. "Popcorn and chocolate!" She pressed her hands together in a pleading motion.

Bree nodded and looked at Penny.

"Churro." She handed Bree a wad of cash, her expression serious. "If they have dipping sauces, get one of each."

There was a reason Penny was her favorite roommate—no offense to Amy—and this was it.

Money in hand, Bree made her way back up the endless steps of the arena, wondering what in the world had possessed designers of basketball facilities to do this to its fans. At least they weren't up in the nosebleeds, she supposed, but it wasn't that much of a consolation.

Thankfully, the line at the nearest concession stand was short, and Bree was able to survey the menu for only a few minutes before it was her turn. Much longer and she might have been swayed to get more than the churro she had set out to get.

She grinned as she saw the pile of dipping sauces for Penny, and she wished she'd thought to bring her jacket so she'd have pockets to carry them in. Thankfully, they slid a bag across the surface too.

Trying to get out of the way of others, Bree loaded up the package of candy atop the popcorn, where the edges of the bag would keep it from falling, and put the churros in one hand; she'd have to use spare fingers and balance for the five different dipping sauces.

She'd look crazy, but that was fine. Nobody she knew would judge her for this anyway.

Turning from the stand, Bree started her way back towards her section, focusing on the food in her hands with the intensity she usually saved for Ryker's baseball games or her school projects.

This, unfortunately, led her to almost slam into a very tall man in a group of other tall men.

"Oh, heavens, I am so sorry," she managed, fumbling awkwardly with trying to put the sauces in the bag the stand had given her.

"No sweat, pet," came his easy reply. He caught one of the sauces as it tumbled off of the others. "Whoa there! Got your hands full, don'tcha?"

Once, Bree might have been embarrassed by the statement, but now she just smiled and let him help put the sauces in the bag. "So would you, if there were five dipping sauces for fresh churros."

She finally looked up at him and nearly swallowed her tongue. The tall, tanned, gorgeously featured blond-haired, blue-eyed, white-teethed man with exceptional shoulders was grinning, but that grin faded quickly as her words sunk in. "They have *what?*"

Then he was gone, brushing by her to the concession stand, his friends laughing almost deliriously after him.

"Mario!" one of them called. Then he chuckled and stepped forward to Bree, his unruly sandy hair almost falling into gray eyes. "Sorry, ma'am. Mario's Canadian, and I'm not sure he's quite grasped the rules of politeness."

The darkest of the guys whacked this one on the arm. "Hey! I thought Canadians were nicer than Americans, Fig."

"Then I have no explanation whatsoever." Fig winked at Bree, which made her smile, not that she felt particularly flirted with, but she felt more like she was with the Six Pack.

Which left only one conclusion.

"And what sport do you all play?" she asked without any hesitation whatsoever.

A few sets of eyes widened, and they all smiled. "How'd you figure that, ma'am?" the one who had hit the other asked, sliding his hands easily into well-worn jeans.

Bree raised a brow. "Wild guess. And experience with this bizarre pack mentality. Rivals a fraternity, resembles a family, right? Gotta be a team, and if I'd hazard another guess, I'd bet you're either minors or pros, whatever your sport is. Dressed too nicely for college, too fit to be pickup, and that one's still got red in his cheeks. It's not cold, so you must have had practice earlier."

"Where did you come from, and are there more of you

there?" a third one asked, darker than the rest and grinning with a knowing smile that could have made any girl a bit dizzy.

Just not Bree.

She grinned right back. "I came from section 102, and there are two others there. But if you want food, get it now; the churros won't last long."

"She just invited us along," Fig stage-whispered to the others.

"Does she know how dangerous that could be?" the dark one whispered back.

"Maybe she's a fangirl," the other joined in.

Bree laughed now. "Not a fangirl, don't know any of you, and I'm not about to be particularly impressed. My brother's an athlete, and I know the type all too well. You're safe with me, and I promise I am safe with you."

The nearest one, who had hit the other, leaned closer, trying for a seductive look and failing. "And how do you know?"

"Because she's a Six Pack Sib, Junior," a new voice announced. "She's got her own security team on speed dial."

Bree turned, and her mouth dropped open without shame. "Clint?"

His very McCarthy-brother grin was fixed in place, lopsided and eye-crinkling, and the sight of it did a funny thing to her stomach. "Hiya, Bree."

"Holy crap!" Without thinking, she shoved the food into Fig's hands and practically ran to Clint, throwing her arms around his neck while he picked her up in the biggest bear hug she'd had in years. "How did I completely forget that you were here?"

Clint groaned and put her back down. "Because I'm a complete loser and didn't claim a dinner when I first got to town. My bad, I owe you."

Bree rolled her eyes and stepped back. "Yeah, cuz it's not like you're busy or anything, Mr. Pro-Hockey Stud." She glanced down at his shirt, then flicked her eyes back up, smiling further. "Nice shirt."

He looked at it, then at hers, and laughed once. "You too."

"Fido, this is adorable, but could we please have some introductions?" Fig called out.

"Fido?" Bree mouthed, raising a brow.

"Later," Clint muttered, turning her to the others so they were side by side, their Belltown shirts proudly blazing. "Bree, that's Jack Hotchkiss, Ryan Figaro, Jimmy Rodgers, and Cal Watterson. Maurice Reynolds is at concessions. Hotch, Fig, Junior, Cal, and Mario."

Bree snorted to herself. "I can figure all of that out except for Mario. What's the deal there?"

"First day on the ice, he comes in wearing a Mario T-shirt, and Coach couldn't remember his name." Cal shrugged. "Called him Mario, and it stuck."

"Figures."

Clint cleared his throat. "Guys, this is Bree Stone."

Two pairs of brows shot up, while her name had no impact on the rest. "As in Ryker 'Rabbit' Stone?" Fig asked in an almost-reverent tone.

"That's the one," Clint replied. "And no, she will not get you his autograph."

Fig's face flushed as the others gave him some good old-fashioned ribbing.

"Thanks," Bree told Clint quietly.

He gave her a brief wink. "I got you."

Only then did Bree realize that Fig held all of the food she'd just bought for herself and the others. Her cheeks heated. "I'm so sorry, Fig. Let me take those back."

She took them before he could say anything resembling a refusal. "No probs," he said easily, whatever starstruck attitude Ryker's name had given him gone now. "I think you've tempted me to get a churro myself. What're the sauces?"

"Cream cheese icing, chocolate, chocolate caramel, white chocolate peanut butter, and salted caramel," she recited, not bothering to hide how hard it was to recall them. "My roommate wants to try them all."

Fig grunted in evident satisfaction. "As well she should. I'm getting some stuff. You guys going with Bree?"

"Is there room?" Clint asked her. "You are literally the only person I know in St. Louis that isn't on my team."

That was oddly adorable, and Bree smiled at him. "There's room. A row of at least eight empty seats behind me and the girls. We can fit you all."

"Perfect!" Cal clapped, then rubbed his hands together. "Let's goooooooo, Lumberjacks!"

"No," Bree and Clint said together, making each other laugh.

"What?" Cal cried out, looking between them both. "I can cheer for them!"

"Not like that," Clint told him. "Come on, you'll hear how it goes." He took the churro sauces from Bree without asking and gestured for her to lead. "After you, Breezy."

Bree shook her head, grinning helplessly at him. "It's really good to see you, Clint."

He smiled back. "Same to you. We gotta catch up."

She eyed him for only a moment, the thought sinking in with some serious resolution. "Yeah," she agreed with a nod. "Yeah, we do."

FOUR

BREE STONE HAD never looked like that.

She couldn't have.

Bree Stone was just a kid, a teenager with her nose in a book that only came down when her brother was at bat. A funny kid, for sure, and a favorite of the entire Six Pack.

She was *not* a stunning beauty that stopped him in his tracks and had worked over his teammates in three minutes flat just by being herself.

Except the moment Clint had seen her, he'd known exactly who it was.

Somehow that only made it better.

As he followed her to the seats at the MSSL arena, his hands still holding the insane amount of dipping sauces for the churros, Clint's mind raced. He needed to calm down, be himself—but cooler than himself—except not too cool, because Bree knew him.

Bree knew him.

Well, sort of. They'd been awkwardly grouped with the other siblings of the Six Pack madness, and that tended to form a bond when in the same place at the same time. Siblings in the spotlight left the others without any attention, and it was a strange feeling.

Clint and Rachel had been closest in age of the group, along with Levi's brother, Rhett. Bree had been a few years younger but had always been around, so her age hadn't really come up among the group. Axel's sister, Silvia, was the youngest, but she was still occasionally in touch, mostly when Axel did something only other Six Pack Sibs would understand. Sylvia's texts were always hilarious, but it had been a while since she'd sent something out.

Rachel was now Clint's sister-in-law, so he saw her all the time, and she had a completely different set of problems being a Six Pack spouse. Rhett was doing computer programming somewhere, and he'd set up their online group, usually moderating from wherever he was. Clint hadn't seen him in years, but they messaged pretty regularly.

Which pretty much left him and Bree.

Bree and him.

They'd both worn Belltown shirts despite not being Belltown alums. They were almost the same shirt too. His was two years older than hers, and that was all.

They were both in St. Louis. Had he remembered she was here? Had someone mentioned that?

He felt strand after strand of connection forging between Bree and him as they walked, though she wouldn't know anything about it. She was the only person outside of his team he knew here, and he was seizing upon that. He would take every advantage of that.

Would he do that if she hadn't grown so incredibly attractive since he'd seen her last?

No clue.

Did it matter?

Probably.

FACEOFF

"Okay, here we go, guys," Bree announced with a tilt of her dark ponytail. "And I apologize for my roommates."

Clint and the others chuckled. "Why?" Clint asked, following behind her as his teammates moved into the row just behind.

Bree glanced over her shoulder with a wince. "Well..."

"Holy crap!"

Clint coughed in surprise at the completely suggestive tone.

Two girls stared at the newcomers with gaping jaws. The taller one, a blond, reached for the popcorn and chocolate from Bree, but her eyes never left Cal. The shorter redhead scanned the rest in succession.

No one looked at Clint.

Except Bree.

"Bree," the redhead gasped. "Babes. You brought all the goods back from concessions. How much do I owe you, and would you like it in tens or twenties?"

Bree's cheeks flamed and she turned to Clint, grabbing the sauces without meeting his eyes, then shoving them into her roommate's hands. "Sauces. Cream cheese, chocolate, chocolate caramel, white chocolate peanut butter, salted caramel."

"Eeny meeny miney moe," came the breathy reply. "Hi, hotties. I'm Penny."

"I'm Amy," the blond one said to no one at all, a glazed-over look falling across her features.

Cal, ever the social butterfly, sat in his seat and leaned forward, hand extended. "Hi there. Cal Watterson."

Penny seemed to snap out of her daze, her eyes going wide. "The hockey player?"

Cal grinned crookedly. "The very same. You find yourself surrounded by a swarm of Hawks, ladies. That okay?"

Penny scoffed and waved a hand. "Swarm away, babe. Sit, sit—we're getting stares."

And like that, they all sat and chatted without hesitation.

Bree looked at her roommates, at Clint's teammates, then at Clint. "That was mortifying."

Clint grinned and shook his head. "Don't worry about it. The guys love attention, and they're used to it." He nudged Bree just a little. "Kind of like traveling with the Pack, right?"

As he'd hoped, Bree rolled her eyes and settled into her seat. "Very much so. I swear, it's like being with a rock star whenever I go out with my brother."

"Same. I don't mind being the 'other' McCarthy brother, if it saves me from that attention."

"Dude! Jack Hotchkiss! Oh, no way, and Fig too!"

Clint winced and leaned forward, rubbing his hands over his face. "And that attention."

The crowd around them began to realize who was among them, and soon autographs and selfies were being requested.

Not from Clint, of course, but his teammates were being bombarded.

"Good grief," Bree muttered, leaning forward to match him and leaning closer as she was jostled. "Is it always like this?"

Clint shrugged. "Can't say we've done that much outside of practice and games, and I haven't played yet, so . . . "

"Why not? I thought Ryker said they wanted you to start right away."

"They do, but they wanted me to get into a rhythm with the team first."

Bree frowned at that, her brow furrowing. "That doesn't sound typical. Don't they normally just toss you in and say, 'Ready, go,' and you deal with it?"

"Pretty much," he admitted, applauding with the crowd

over something happening on the court. "Coach Singleton is a little different. He likes a cohesive team and focuses on building that rather than just having players out on the ice. The season is still early, so he wants me to build a rapport with my line before I'm in it."

"And how's that working out?"

Clint smirked and jerked a thumb behind him. "Hotch and Fig are my wings."

Bree glanced behind him, then snickered. "Oh boy. Lucky you."

"Yep. Winning."

He watched as she slowly rubbed her hands together, her attention now on the game. "Ryker said he and the guys are coming out for a game."

Clint nodded, trying to focus on the game himself despite his attention wanting nothing more than to stay with Bree. He could handle a bit of distraction for a while, if for no other reason than to rearrange his mind back to its usual function.

"Yeah," he said when he realized he hadn't answered her. "Grizz says they're all coming out next week." He shrugged. "It'll be great to have them, but it's not like I'll be able to enjoy it."

Bree gave him a sidelong look. "Why's that? You know them; they'll take you out after the game and make a big fuss."

"Right, right, and then what?" He glanced at her, raising a brow. "Before, the focus would have been all on them. Now?" He pointed a finger at himself.

"Ohhhh. Ick." Bree made a face that had Clint chuckling. She was one of the only people that would have that reaction, and he loved it.

"Uh-huh."

"You don't want to be the next big thing?"

He shook his head, still smiling. "Nope. Well, if I earn it, maybe. But not as an accessory to the Six Pack, you know? And having them be there is just going to drag the spotlight over to me, and what's that going to do except bring attention to my playing?"

A roar from the crowd around them pulled them both back to the game on the court for a moment, his teammates roaring with approval behind them.

Clint checked the scoreboard, grunting at the tied numbers. "Doesn't look like either team is running away with this one."

"Clint."

He looked back over at Bree, who was giving him a very bemused look. "What's that for?"

She smiled, almost like she was laughing at him, but just to herself. "You're a professional athlete, and now you're playing at the highest level. You're going to get attention, and probably a lot of fans."

"I know, it's just . . . " He sighed, fighting for the words that he hadn't confided to anyone yet. "I just want to play, Bree. I've always just wanted to play."

"You are playing, and you will be playing. You just get to be on TV now." She nudged him, making him smirk. "Smile for the cameras, Clint."

He rolled his eyes, forcing a grimacing grin for effect. "Cheese . . . "

Bree nodded in apparent approval. "Very good. Put that on the cover of *Sports Monthly*."

"Will do."

"Nah, Fido's a page-six piece. Maybe a footnote."

Clint looked up at Mario wryly as his teammate reappeared with armfuls of food. "At least I make the issue, Mario. When was the last time you did anything noteworthy?"

The guys crowed with appreciation at that, nudging and razzing each other to the delight of anyone around them.

"What was that you were saying about being part of the team?" Bree asked him with a smile as she took a bite of her churro.

"These clowns?" He glanced back at his teammates, then at Bree again. "Nah. It's easy to horse around with them. That comes with dying on the ice together. But I'm not worried about the rest of it. It'll come together, and we'll see what happens when it does."

Bree raised a brow as she swallowed. "That's very fortune cookie of you. You believe it?"

Clint laughed, then made a face. "If I say it enough, I just might. But enough about me. What about you? How's school?"

"Why does everyone ask that?" Bree mused aloud, heaving a sigh that he didn't understand. "It's the strangest question. How's school? Well, the buildings are falling over, but we've been doing drills, so . . . "

"I hate when buildings fall."

She gave him a look. "Funny. Do you want to know about my grades? My program? My social life? I've been recently quizzed on this by Ryker, Trista, and my parents, so my answers are prepped."

He hadn't expected this, and he found himself mentally backpedaling faster than he could physically backpedal. "Uhhh . . . just a question. If you don't want to answer that, pick another."

"Ask me how my churro is."

He snorted a laugh but turned to her and plastered a polite smile on his face. "How is your churro, Bree?"

She shrugged a shoulder. "Not bad. Pretty good for concession-stand food, but I've had better." She smiled with what seemed to be real amusement, which made him want to laugh, which made even the conversation about churros significant. "You want to try some?"

Habit told him to politely decline, to let her continue to enjoy it alone and to keep going with the awkward yet polite conversation he was enjoying so much, but mischief outbid habit this time. Clint ripped off the top bit of churro and popped it into his mouth, nodding in thought as he chewed. "Not half bad."

Bree giggled and covered her face with one hand. "Oh my gosh, Clint."

"What?" he asked around the mouthful of churro. "You offered."

"I know, but I didn't think you'd . . . Never mind." She dropped her hand and grinned at him. "What else do you want to ask me?"

What else? At least a thousand and three questions just to figure out who the girl he had known had become and why he was so fascinated with her. What she'd been doing since they'd seen each other last, whenever that had been, and what she was doing now. What she wanted to do, where she wanted to go, and strangely enough, if she knew anything at all about hockey.

He didn't know if he wanted her to know a lot or nothing at all.

"Will you come to my first game next week?"

Wait, what? Why was that the question that had come out of his mouth? He wanted her to come, absolutely, but he'd been planning to work up to that, maybe get the invitation in by the end of the night.

Definitely not in the first hour of seeing her again.

But he couldn't take it back, so he sat there like an idiot, staring at her with a mixture of terror and hope.

Bree's smile was surprisingly soft, her hazel eyes almost dancing. "Yeah."

Clint gaped, his mouth literally falling open. "Really? You'll come?"

Now Bree laughed, tearing off another piece of churro and gesturing with it. "Sure!" she said, plopping the churro piece into her mouth, somehow still smiling while chewing it.

There was something he didn't quite trust about that smile. Her answer had come too easily, not that it was a big deal to come to a hockey game, of all things. Bree didn't know him all that well anymore, really, despite the current feeling of renewed friendship and new interest.

Something was up.

Clint narrowed his eyes at her. "Ryker already invited you, didn't he?"

Bree's smile slowly spread to a grin, tension in his chest tightening with every degree. "Yep."

Of course he had. Clint shook his head. "Unbelievable."

"Sorry." Bree shrugged. "This way he combines a visit to see you with a visit to see me. He's opportunistic."

That was one way of putting it, but Clint wasn't about to let Ryker take the victory out of Clint's first game before a single goal was scored.

He quirked his brows. "So am I." He tugged his phone out of his back pocket and waved it at Bree. "Time for a Six Pack selfie?"

"Absolutely." On cue, Bree scooted closer, and Clint's throat dried unexpectedly.

Bree Stone making his throat dry.

Absolutely bizarre.

Swallowing against the Sahara, Clint held up his phone, framing himself and the beautiful woman beside him perfectly into frame. "Smile or silly?" he heard himself ask, his pulse leaping as she brushed against his arm, the cinnamon-infused lavender scent of her dancing in his senses.

"Both," Bree said firmly, smiling at the camera.

"'Kay." Forcing himself to smile, he snapped a picture, willing himself not to blink at the image of the two of them smiling together.

Good grief, he was losing his mind.

"Okay, have at," he ordered, more at himself than at Bree.

What followed was a series of at least seven stupid faces between the pair of them, pictures occurring for each one and a few times between. They laughed at each of them, Bree insisted he delete at least three, and he only deleted one. He did let her pick which stupid one went to the guys, and then they sat waiting, staring at his phone.

Anyone else seeing them would have thought they were phone addicts or completely uninterested in the basketball game. They were, but not for the reasons other people thought.

If there was one thing any Six Pack Sib knew, it was that none of the guys was ever far from their phone, and responses would rapidly fly once they began.

Yet again, they did not disappoint.

Axel: BREE!

Sawyer: Breezy!

Cole: Who's the ugly guy with my little sister?

Grizz: It's Bree!

Ryker: Dawg, she's not your sister.

Ryker: Hi, sis!

Levi: Oh look, all, it's what's-his-name!

Clint scowled playfully at the phone. "Why do they like you more than me?"

"Aww, feeling left out?" she teased, typing out a quick reply on her phone.

"Kinda, yeah."

Bree: Hi, boys!

Cole: What are you doing with that guy?

Clint: Thanks, guys. Thanks a lot. Might need to change my shirt now.

Sawyer: DON'T YOU DARE.

Axel: You wouldn't...

Grizz: I'll disown you.

Bree: Wow, defensive much? We're proudly repping a school we didn't even go to.

Sawyer: The shirt is great, we love it. It's your date we question.

Clint coughed in surprise, shaking his head. "Unreal, absolutely unreal."

Bree rolled her eyes at him. "Come on, you knew it was going there. They have the maturity of thirteen-year-olds."

"True, but still." He glanced behind him at his teammates, then leaned closer to Bree. "Don't tell Fig we're texting your brother. He might cry."

She snorted a soft laugh, returning her attention to the phone.

Ryker: Yeah, this isn't what I meant when I said I wanted you to get out more.

Bree: We are NOT having that conversation on here!

Axel: Maybe we should.

Cole: Yeah, if you're out with Clint, we def should.

Bree: Be nice to Clint, we just bumped into each other.

Levi: And he doesn't have any friends, right?

"Are you guys texting each other while sitting next to each other?" Hotch asked, leaning between the two of them. "That's totes adorbs."

Bree leaned back to look up at him in dismay. "What are you, a fourteen-year-old girl?"

"Yes!" Cal cheered, then leaned forward to wrap his arms

around Bree's shoulders from behind. "Thank you, thank you, you are my new favorite person in the entire world."

Clint shook his head in mock shame and embarrassment. "Amazing. Absolutely amazing, I can't take you guys anywhere."

Bree, laughing her head off, patted Cal's arms gently. "Glad I could make your day, Cal." She tossed a smile back to Hotch. "I didn't hurt your feelings, did I?"

Hotch grinned back at her. "Nah. I like a girl who can put me in my place. Full points."

Bree saluted him with two fingers as Cal released her, then looked directly at Clint.

Who, for some reason, had forgotten that he shouldn't stare at her so openly. Especially when other people were talking, his phone was blowing up, and there was a game going on.

Whoops.

"What?" Bree asked slowly, a small, crooked smile appearing.

Clint could only shake his head again. "It's just great to see you. Really great."

Her brow furrowed just a little, her smile not moving. "You said that already."

"I know." He let himself smile further. "It's that true."

For the first time, he saw a hint of pink race into her cheeks, and she turned her attention to the game. He watched her swallow and felt an entirely male jolt of satisfaction at it.

Why was that? Why did making Bree embarrassed or uncomfortable or whatever it was make him want to smile more?

She hadn't moved away from him after the photos, and she wasn't moving away now.

"You wanna grab a bite to eat after the game?" Bree asked without looking at him.

Now Clint did smile, still watching her. "Of course. I think the guys are going to want to take us all out, though."

Bree nodded. "I meant this game."

What the...

YES.

"Absolutely," he told her without hesitation.

Again, Bree nodded, her attention on the court.

Clint watched the game too, but his attention was on her.

It couldn't go anywhere else.

FIVE

"Bree Insert-Middle-Name Stone, you've got some 'splainin' to do."

Bree blinked hard at her roommate as she stumbled out of her bedroom. "I what?"

Penny sat cross-legged on their couch in her sweats and a faded high school T-shirt, glasses in place, hair piled up in a bun on top of her head. Her ever-present mug of coffee sat on the table, her laptop propped next to it, work clearly happening.

Or it had been up until Bree entered the scene.

"Ahem."

Bree flicked her eyes up to the stubborn redhead. "Yeah?"

Penny raised a brow. "I can count on no hands at all how many times you have come home after eleven, babe. I know we're not besties, but I do consider myself the mom of this place. Get your butt over here and spill the beans."

"About what?" Bree asked evasively, moving to the kitchen and heading straight for the coffee pot. She wasn't a huge coffee drinker, but if an inquisition was on the way, she would need it.

"Oh, please. How about Captain Blue Eyes and his amazing lats of steel?"

A startled coughing fit attacked Bree with a ferocity that she was entirely unprepared for.

Captain Blue Eyes?

They were a startling color, actually. Gorgeous, to be precise. Clint had always been an attractive guy—anybody could see that—but teenage Bree hadn't really thought of him that way. She hadn't ever considered him anything but Grizz's brother. Just part of the Six Pack package, really. They'd shared the longsuffering looks only Six Pack Sibs would get, joked and laughed, occasionally shared messages with the others, but that was about it.

It had never been just the two of them.

But last night . . .

Something had possessed her, something brave and fiery that knocked aside awkward, insecure Bree Stone and invited the handsome, charming, funny, and yes, impeccably built Clint McCarthy out to dinner after the basketball game last night. His emphatic answer had sent a full-on swarm of butterflies into her stomach, as well as turning her lips almost completely numb and buzzing, making her wonder if she had suddenly developed an allergy to churros.

Somehow, he had gotten them away from his teammates without anybody saying something embarrassing, while she had simply said "I'll see you at home" to her roommates.

She hadn't missed the looks they'd given each other, and her, but she'd written that off as curiosity, since she'd never so much as spent twenty minutes in the company of a guy in front of them before. They had never met any of her ill-fated dates, and she wasn't the sort of girl to gush about guys.

And she wouldn't start now.

"Your silence speaks volumes."

Bree glanced over at Penny as she poured coffee for herself. "My silence says, 'It's morning, need coffee.' Don't read into it."

"Uh-huh." Penny folded her arms, her lips twisting in disgruntlement. "Where did the pair of you go?"

Sighing, Bree set the coffee pot back and began opening cupboards. "You aren't going to stop, are you?"

"Huh-uh. Creamer's in the fridge, cinnamon top shelf in the cupboard on your left."

"Thanks." Bree paused, looking at Penny in shock. "How did you know how I drink my coffee?"

Penny grinned and shrugged. "I'm in public relations. It's my job to notice things."

That wasn't exactly true, but considering Penny's background in advertising, Bree suspected it was more habit and experience that made her pick up tiny details.

"Right." Bree grabbed the cinnamon and moved to the fridge, grabbing the creamer and a yogurt.

"Still not letting go. My group project rescheduled, so I have alllllllll morning."

Of course she did.

Bree groaned, closing her eyes for a second before resuming her coffee preparations. "Mama's Pancakes. We went to Mama's Pancakes."

"Excellent cinnamon rolls there." Penny shifted on the couch, turning to face her. "What'd you get? What did he get? I've always wondered what hockey guys eat."

"That's the sort of thing you wonder?" Bree asked with a laugh, returning the creamer to the fridge. "Food, Penny. They eat food."

Penny barked a very fake laugh. "Funny. What did the gorgeous specimen order, Bree? Dang, it's like pulling teeth to get the details."

"I'm private!" Bree opted to sit at their secondhand kitchen table rather than join Penny on the couch, if for no other reason than to give herself some distance from her roommate. And this conversation.

Now Penny gave her a look. "I'm not exactly going to post all this to the internet, hon. I'm just invested. I thought your cheeks were gonna break with how much you were smiling. It was so cute."

Bree's cheeks flamed on cue, and she sipped her still-too-hot coffee, singeing her tongue. She knew full well she had smiled a lot; she'd shoved a pillow in her face for an hour last night just remembering what an idiot she had been all night in that regard. At the game alone, she had been all of twelve years old with Clint, but at dinner, she'd actually hurt her face smiling and laughing.

And she hadn't faked a moment of it.

Being with Clint had simply been that great. That entertaining. That fun.

Whatever awkwardness she'd felt at the game and sitting there beside him, at dinner, when it was just the two of them, it had been like they were back at a dinner at Belltown, where they had been designated to the siblings' table. They'd flat out judged and speculated about other guests in the restaurant, stolen from each other's plates, and swapped sibling horror stories in recent years. He'd shared funny stories about his time while deployed, she'd given him a taste of what going to college close to her parents had been like.

She hadn't laughed that much in years.

Literally, it had been years.

"He got the breakfast sampler," Bree heard herself admit, thinking back to the night before. "I got cinnamon pancakes and a milkshake."

"A milkshake?" Penny laughed, dropping her head onto the back of the couch. "Of course you did. What did he say?"

Bree smiled. "He complained he didn't know that was an option."

"And you said?"

"Tough."

"Attagirl!" Penny applauded, then mocked bowing down to Bree before sitting back. "So? Did he kiss you?"

Bree's jaw dropped. "What? No! Oh my gosh, why would you . . . ? We're just friends, Penny! We've been friends for years, and we were just catching up! It wasn't a date!"

Penny's mouth formed a thin line, and her eyes narrowed. "Did he pay?"

"Yes . . . " Bree admitted with all the reluctance she could drum up.

"And you decided you were going before the second half, right?"

Bree bit the inside of her lip hard. "Yeah . . . "

"And it was just the two of you?"

"You know it was."

"Planned ahead," Penny pointed out, holding up a finger. "Paired off. Paid for." She waved the now-three fingers in Bree's direction. "A date by anyone's definition."

Bree turned to her yogurt and moodily tore off the top, frowning when it didn't come off cleanly, an annoying corner staying put. "A date is not a proposal."

"Did I say it was? Good night, girl, get over it. Sorry I asked about a kiss. I just saw how often you were looking at each other, and I wondered if he decided to do something about it. Or you did."

How often . . . ?

He was looking?

She knew she had been, had spent the drive over to the restaurant berating herself for it, but had he really . . . ?

"He was looking?" Bree asked in a very small voice, her eyes darting back to her roommate with the same hint of hope her heart currently quivered with.

Penny smiled, her eyes bright. "Yep. He looked. I almost paid the arena-camera guys to put you two on Kiss Cam just to cut the tension I was feeling."

"Penny!" Bree propped her elbow on the table, her forehead going into one hand. "Oh my gosh. How am I going to do this?"

"Do what?" Penny demanded, eagerly sitting up. "What's next?"

Bree would have given a lot of money to say nothing, but the truth of the matter was that part of her was dying to tell someone. Not that it was a surprise, but given last night . . . Well, it felt like something.

"I'm going to his game next week," Bree told her, scooping yogurt onto her spoon. "The Six Pack are coming to town, and Ryker invited me along."

Penny sat in silence for a second. "Your brother invited you? Not Clint?"

Biting her lip, Bree fought a smile. "No . . . Clint invited me too."

"Bree!" Penny squealed, slapping the couch.

"What?" she laughed. "My brother invited me first, so I was already going to go, and then Clint asked if I would come, so . . . " She trailed off, shrugging. "He seemed happy I was coming."

"Of course he was!" Penny shook her head, probably thinking Bree was a naïve little idiot about all of this, but she wasn't saying so. "And what are you two doing after?"

Bree waved her hand as she ate her yogurt. "Oh, the Six Pack will take us all out. That's tradition."

"Oh." Penny sat back, her face falling with irritation and disappointment.

That, for some reason, was hysterical.

"Six of the most sought-after professional baseball players are taking us out to eat, and you're upset?" Bree laughed, falling back against the back of her chair. "That's the greatest thing ever!"

"Hey!" Penny protested. "I'm just really focused on Team Brint right now. I don't care that much about the Glorious Six."

That stopped Bree's laughter in its tracks. "Team what now?"

Her roommate's brows quirked. "Brint. It's better than Clee, don't you think?"

"Marginally." Bree swallowed hard, her mouth completely dry. "Why?"

"Because I'm bored," Penny said bluntly, picking up her laptop. "I might as well ship the two of you while I've got a front-row seat. Besides, he's got some really cute teammates, and I wouldn't mind getting that side dish while you enjoy main course."

That wasn't particularly comforting.

A soft dinging met Bree's ears, and she pulled her phone out of the pocket of her flannel pajama pants.

One new message.

Why did that make her heart skip?

"Tell Clint I said good morning," Penn called airily, sipping her coffee as annoyingly loud as possible.

Bree couldn't even look up as she opened the message.

Clint: Last night was great! Not sure the sampler will be a good idea halfway through practice today, but the company was perfect. Heard there's a great pizza place on your campus. Meet me there later?

A strange sound thundered a steady pattern in her ears, deafening anything else and creating an equally bizarre pressure behind her eyes as she stared at the words on the screen. She couldn't blink, couldn't think, could barely comprehend what she was reading.

THUMP-thump . . . THUMP-thump . . . THUMP-thump . . .

She swallowed, and the sound of her own heart faded just enough for her to regain a grain of sanity and sense.

Glancing surreptitiously at Penny, who was apparently absorbed in her work again, Bree's thumbs flew across the keypad of her screen.

Bree: Sure thing!

No, no exclamation points. She couldn't be *that* eager.

She deleted it quickly.

Bree: Sure thing. Let me know when you're free, if you're not dead.

She pressed her teeth into her tongue, waiting with more anxiety than she'd felt outside of the testing center of the university during finals week.

Another soft ding, and she bit back a gasp of relief.

Clint: Dead? Excuse me, I'm a professional. I've never died in practice a day in my life.

Bree laughed to herself and considered a response before typing back.

"And she's a goner," Penny said to no one in particular, sighing dramatically.

Bree's only response was a slightly amused hum and then to sip her still-warm coffee while she waited for another text response.

SIX

THE CROWD DRUMMED their feet and clapped their hands to the beat of the music blaring from the speakers, every seat filled, nothing but a sea of black and purple. Faces were streaked with the colors like war paint, and team banners waved proudly from the raised arms. The noise rolled like thunder across the entire arena, echoing off of every possible surface and drowning out any coherent thought.

This was exactly what made his heart pound and his blood race. This was exactly how he loved to play and exactly what he needed.

Clint skated around their half of the rink with his teammates, his helmet unstrapped, looking up into the stands, grinning at the sight. He hadn't played in an arena this full since the Northbrook days, and even then, intense as it had been, it couldn't compare with this. His heart thudded against his ribcage in perfect time with the crowd's stomping, the handle of his stick barely registering as a sensation against his glove.

It almost never did; it was an extension of him, not a

piece of equipment. It responded to his every move and did exactly as it was told, and most of the time, he didn't even remember he had it.

Now it glided along with him, hovering just above the ice. He glanced at the tip of it, curved to the perfect degree with his treatment, wrapped in tape where it needed to be, crisp and seeming to glint in the lights above them. This was their moment, their night on the ice before this eager crowd.

The big time.

He'd made it.

Now to not throw up or make a fool of himself.

Nerves were part of what made intense games worth it, and he was used to playing through them without an issue, so it wasn't as though he expected any disastrous results.

Worth considering, though.

The chanting of the crowd suddenly became clearer, the words pounding in his head.

"Hawks! Hawks! Hawks!"

His head bobbed absently along with it, his eyes raising to scan the crowd.

They hadn't told him where they were sitting, but he knew they'd make themselves known . . .

On cue, a wave started midway up the stands right at center ice, rippling around the entire arena with perfection. But at the beginning of that wave, signs suddenly shot up, each one with a single letter.

G-O F-I-D-O.

Clint coughed in surprise, the sign holders literally roaring incoherently, seeing him looking up at them.

There they were, in all their glory, and a few phones suddenly raised in their directions. There was no mistaking the Six Pack wherever they went.

"Nice fan club, Fido," Hook commented with a nudge as he passed him.

"Thanks," Clint muttered, shaking his head, unable to keep from grinning. He wet his lips, laughing to himself as he circled around once more.

Those guys . . .

He looked up again, focusing more intently.

Grizz had the last letter, and he pointed directly at Clint as he whooped, Rachel standing beside him, hands pressed together at her chin. If he knew Rach, she was probably tearing up like his mom. Flicking his eyes one person over, his mom was beaming and waving like any mom in the stands would, no matter what level her kid plays at.

Yep, she was crying.

Typical.

The whole McCarthy clan had made the trip out, including his nieces and nephews, three of whom were likely wearing headphones in this noise.

Madness. Absolute madness.

Oh well.

He looked at the whole group of them again as the wave started there once more, the *G* sign dipping enough to show a white-blond flash of hair.

That'd be Rabbit.

Which meant . . .

Pulse skipping one notch, Clint glanced to Ryker's right. Sporting a purple T-shirt, dark hair loose around her shoulders, was Bree.

Her eyes locked on his, and he smiled again just for her. He loved that everyone was here, but for some reason, she was the one he wanted there the most.

He needed to signal that he saw her, that he was happy to see her, that he was ready for this . . .

She'd never see his face with his helmet on and from this distance.

He'd never really set up a signal with his family over the years; he'd always just nodded.

Would she get that?

Swallowing a random wash of nerves, he just thumped his hand over his heart with his free hand twice and pointed his fist up at the entire gang. At Bree to start, then running down the length of them.

They cheered louder, but he saw Bree mimic the action before turning to say something to her brother.

No matter how this game turned out, he'd already won something.

The buzzer overhead sounded, and Clint returned his attention to the ice. Warmups were over. It was time for the intros.

He exhaled slowly, skating towards the box with the rest of his team. They'd only have a few minutes in the locker room with the coaches before they were lining up for their big intros.

Hook stood at the box, clapping each player on the back like the captain he was as they exited the ice and headed for the locker room.

Clint barely felt it. Barely heard anyone say anything to him. Barely felt the seat beneath him as he sat at his locker.

He wanted to get back out there. Wanted the feel of the ice beneath his skates. Wanted to meet his opponent at center ice and stare him down as though it were a battle to the death.

The Nashville Hounds were a great team, and he'd studied film for hours on them in preparation for this game.

He was more than ready, and waiting was going to kill him.

Memories from his time on the ice flashed through his mind. Playoff games as a kid, tournaments with Northbrook, practices where his legs had actually given out on him from fatigue . . . Great shots he'd made on goal, trick plays, the feel of racing down the ice unimpeded by anybody on his way to scoring . . .

His entire hockey career in a highlight reel right there before him. All culminating in his performance on the ice tonight, whatever it was. This was the start of something big, and he couldn't wait to get it going. Hockey had been everything since he had gotten home from tour. There was no backup plan. There was nothing else.

Just hockey. Just him, the puck, and the ice.

This was it.

"Dude, didn't you play with Zamboni back in the day?"

Clint blinked and looked up at Mario as the rest of the guys were getting up from their lockers.

Had he missed the whole pep talk from Coach?

Great . . .

"Fido?"

He shook himself. "What? Zamboni?"

"Zane Winchester?" Mario said with wide eyes. "Cheese and crackers, Fido, wake up! The guy's from Chi-town like you are; didn't you play for Northbrook together?"

Clint swallowed, his throat suddenly parched. "Yeah, we did. That was ages ago. Haven't talked to the guy in years."

"Well, Moose is supposed to track him tonight, so any words of wisdom for the guy might be useful." Mario grabbed Clint's pads and practically hoisted him to his feet. "You good, man?"

Clint blinked again, hard, then raised his chin and exhaled once. "I'm good."

Mario didn't look totally convinced, but when Clint said nothing else, Mario slapped his chest. "Let's go, then. And watch out for your boy. He's hungry this year, and he might be going for the penalty box record."

"Sounds like him," Clint muttered, shaking his head.

He'd forgotten all about Zane in his prep for this. He'd seen the guy on film, and he knew full well he played for this team and that he was even more an animal on the ice now than he'd been when they were teenagers.

Somehow it hadn't actually sunk in that they'd be on the ice together.

Didn't matter, but it was a strange feeling all the same.

Clint followed his teammates out of the locker room, wondering how time had passed without him actually noticing when he was this hyped up.

He heard the announcer running through the visiting team, though any names were lost on them this deep beneath the stands. He did manage to hear the crowd booing loudly, and it faintly occurred to him to wonder what that was about.

He bounced on his skates against the rubber of the floor, raring to go.

Come on, come on . . . his mind urged. *Let's get out there, let's go!*

Someone in the lineup was whistling a very western-movie-sounding song, and a few of the guys laughed.

"Knock it off, Chezzy," someone else barked. "I hate that one!"

Chezzy, on cue, switched to whistling the theme song of a very old TV show.

Groans rose from everyone in the lineup.

Clint shook his head, grinning to himself.

Hockey players. They were all the same in so many ways.

The crowd suddenly roared with newfound fervor, and Clint's heart rate skyrocketed. Music blared thunderously, the beat of it ricocheting through the floor, up the skates, and into the chest of every one of them.

One by one, the team shuffled forward as their names were called, skating out onto the ice to the cheers of their home crowd.

Clint stared straight ahead, watching as one by one his teammates went out, inhaling and exhaling slowly as his body literally pulsed with the desire to join them.

Cal was right in front of him, then he was gone, out on the ice and pumping his fists for the crowd.

This was it.

Showtime.

"Playing center, number thirty-three, welcome to St. Louis, Clint McCarthy!"

He pushed off, onto the ice, skating out into the completely dark arena but for the illumination on the ice, a spotlight following him as he raised his stick in greeting. The crowd cheered, a certain section a bit louder than others, but the entire place was roaring for the Hawks in general.

Clint joined his teammates on the blue line, forcing himself to not smile, though all he wanted to do was grin like an idiot. He glanced over at the entrance he'd just come from, nodding to himself at the black and purple flames on the screens beside it. Kinda cool—he wasn't going to pretend it wasn't.

"Welcome to the big time, Fido," Cal said beside him, looking around the arena. "Not a bad gig, huh?"

"Eh," Clint replied with a one-shoulder shrug. "It's all right."

Cal snickered as the rest of the guys joined them and the goalies were announced.

Clint's knees buzzed as they stood there for the national anthem, then seemed to sigh with relief when they left the blue line and headed for the box. The team's telltale screeching hawk cry echoed over the speakers, sending the entire place roaring once more.

The boards were literally shaking as Clint joined the team at the boxes. This was electric, and he loved every insane second.

"All right, boys," Coach said as they came in, the next shifts taking their seats on the benches and grabbing bottles of water.

Clint shook his head when he was offered one. He couldn't think about that. Not yet, not now.

"Long shift to start," Coach was saying. "Outskate them, outthink them, outplay them. Steady game, stay focused. Got it?"

"Yes, Coach!" they answered as one, like the obedient army they were.

Coach nodded at Hook, who cleared his throat. "'Kay, boys, keep your heads, ride the ice. Hawks on three! One, two, three!"

"HAWKS!"

Clint clapped sticks with Hotch and Fig as their line headed out to center ice. He glanced over his shoulder at Moose and Robo on defense and nodded at Chezzy in goal. Chezzy tapped his stick to both poles, then twice on the ice.

"Here we go, Fido," Chezzy bellowed. "Here we go, kid!"

Leaning forward just a touch at his waist, Clint glided towards his place, exhaling slowly through his nose as his opponent did the same. The ref came at them from his right, a flash of white and black in his periphery.

He wouldn't look at him, couldn't take his eyes away from the center for the Hounds.

This was war. At this moment, they were alone in a ring,

the power to change the dynamics of the game in their hands. Nothing started without them.

The two of them would dictate how it began.

He couldn't lose this drop.

He wouldn't.

The puck suddenly came into his line of vision and his eyes immediately tracked it, his stick moving into position on the ice, his right hand sliding lower down the shaft, his left elbow cocking back as that hand steadied the butt end.

Inhale... Exhale... Inhale...

THUMP-thump ... THUMP-thump ... THUMP-thump...

Almost in slow motion, the puck dropped, and the blade of Clint's stick was moving in anticipation.

Clint's breath caught as he felt the pressure of the puck cradling against the stick.

NOW.

He shot the puck immediately over to Fig, who darted past his opponent to receive, while Clint shoved off of his guy to race down the ice.

Fig dribbled the ice for a minute before passing it back to Clint, who scanned the ice quickly, calculating his move in milliseconds before faking a pass back to Fig, then passing to himself between a player's skates when the guy fell for it. He weaved towards the right, dribbling the puck carefully before dropping it back to Hotch as he came up behind him.

Hotch moved to center, then came back towards Clint, passing the puck. "Fido!"

"Here, here!" Clint called, taking it and charging towards the goal, despite the defense.

"Ha! Ha!" came the call from further down.

Without more than a fleeting look, Clint sent the puck in

that direction, grunting when Fig scooped it up and slapped it towards the goal.

The goalie stopped it easily, dropping it to the side of the net to a defender, who immediately took it to the boards.

"Chip!" someone called, and Clint raced over to intercept it.

"Heads up!" Hotch called as he screeched across Clint's left.

Clint barely had time to register the call before he was slammed hard into the boards, something in his body making a cracking sound against the plexiglass, followed by a focused blow to his left cheek.

The whistle blew as the crowd roared in disgust.

"Long time no see," grunted a familiar voice in Clint's ear as the crushing force against him slipped away.

Searing pain erupted across Clint's cheekbone as he groaned, looking at his attacker as play stopped.

Zane Winchester, tall, ripped, and powerful, grinned viciously at Clint while he skated backwards towards the penalty box without waiting for the ref to push him there.

Clint glared at his one-time teammate, spitting weakly onto the ice as he tasted blood.

Zane puckered up in a quick kissing motion, then turned to the penalty box, raising his arms in the air to the booing crowd.

"You good, Fido?" Hotch asked as he skated with him over to the faceoff spot.

"Fine," he spat.

"Cheek's bleeding."

"Yeah." He dabbed at it quickly.

"Dude," Moose grunted as he came to center ice, standing behind center line. "Da heck was that?"

Clint sniffed and spat once more. "Zamboni wanted to say hi, I guess."

Moose glowered darkly. "I got his number now. On your six, Fido." He nodded, then backed up to his position.

Clint blinked, then looked at Hotch. "What just happened? Moose doesn't even like me."

Hotch grinned and chuckled. "Nope, but he really doesn't like people messing with his teammates. Liking you isn't even a factor. His team, his people."

"Huh. Go figure." Clint shook his head and moved over to the faceoff.

His opponent grinned at him as he approached. "Fido, is it?"

"So?" Clint shot back, not particularly inclined to take anybody's trash.

His tone had zero effect. "Charlie Dance. Played you back when I was with the Cyclones."

Clint had no memory of that but nodded anyway. What was with the small talk?

Dance's smile didn't waver a bit. "Welcome to the big leagues." He gestured to his cheek. "You've got something on your face there."

Clint glowered as he got into faceoff position. "Shut up."

SEVEN

WHAT. WAS. THAT?

Bree sat in her brother's rental car, staring straight ahead, barely blinking.

She'd done nothing but go from seated to standing about three thousand and forty-two times in the last few hours, her voice was hoarse from cheering, and her eyes actually hurt from straining to see, even though they'd had good seats.

She'd been to enough sporting events in her life to be pretty good at catching things, but this was another animal entirely.

The speed of that game had left her exhausted and exhilarated and, she admitted, a little lost.

Ryker had talked her through parts, but then they both got so caught up in the game that instruction went out the window. She got the gist of the game, but the specifics were nowhere to be found. Not that it mattered all that much; she just preferred understanding what she was seeing.

How in the world did anyone play anything at the speeds she had seen today?

And Clint . . .

Clint had been amazing.

Her lungs hurt just at that thought, let alone at the memories, and she rubbed at her chest as if that would help.

"Heartburn?" Ryker asked as they pulled into the parking lot.

"Huh?" She shook herself and looked over at him. "What? No, just tired." She forced a smile. "I haven't yelled like that in a long time."

Ryker coughed in mock distress. "What? You don't scream your head off at my games?"

Bree raised a brow at him. "No one screams in baseball the way people screamed tonight."

He seemed to consider that. "I guess that's true. Well, maybe not true, but you certainly feel it more at hockey, huh?"

"Acoustics, if nothing else."

Her brother was silent for a moment. "Man, that was intense. Clint looked great, didn't he?"

"Sure did," she said, maybe too quickly.

Drat.

She looked out of her window, the curve of her index finger flying to her top lip as though she were thinking.

In truth, she was finishing her sentence in silence.

Sure did. He looked REALLY great.

He looked attractive. He looked impressive.

He looked amazing.

By the third part of the game, whatever that was called, she wasn't even trying to pay attention to anyone else on the ice. She only really cared about where Clint was, how Clint was playing, and if anyone else was going to crash him into the side of the rink, whatever *that* was called, like the filthy animal had in the first part.

She'd cheered especially hard when Clint's teammate had

delivered an amazing retaliatory blow to the guy late in the first part of the game. He'd also gotten a penalty for it, but the Hounds hadn't scored during the powerplay, so it was fine.

Powerplay. Of all the terms to remember, that was it?

She was such an amateur.

Like an embarrassing amateur.

She could ask his five-year-old nephew to teach her hockey, and it would be an education.

Rubbing at her brow, she bit back a sigh as Ryker turned into a parking spot. As much as she loved the Six Pack, as great as it had been to hang out with them in the stands tonight, she really didn't want to do this. She didn't want to be at a late-night dinner with a big group, fun as they were. She didn't even want to hang out with the McCarthy clan.

She just wanted to see Clint.

And it scared her that it was all she could think about.

They'd been out three times between the basketball game and tonight, and each time had been fantastic. Nothing monumental, nothing even particularly special. Two days ago, they'd just grabbed some ice cream after she was tired of studying for an exam.

They'd talked for two hours after they'd finished the ice cream.

She had never just talked with anyone like that, especially a guy. She wasn't the most social person, it was true, but she kind of hated talking just for the sake of it.

Talking with Clint didn't feel like talking.

Listening to Clint didn't feel like a chore.

Being with Clint . . .

Well, it wasn't like being with anyone else.

What a flipping cliché.

"Ready?"

Bree nodded and unbuckled her seatbelt, opening her

door and stepping out without a word. How was she going to do this? How was she going to get through this entire crazy meal without putting her foot in her mouth or being noticeably silent or crawling across the table to kiss Clint right on the mouth?

The curb bashed into her toe at that thought, and she stumbled, her brother catching her arm before she could actually fall.

"Whoa there, sis," Ryker laughed, steadying her.

Bree exhaled slowly. *Get it together.* She cleared her throat and grinned at Ryker somehow. "Did you see that curb jump in my way?"

He grinned right back. "Yeah! What gives? Stupid curb should watch where it's going!"

"Honestly." She snorted, even as her heart pounded unsteadily.

That was close.

She felt all of fourteen years old, and she was suddenly desperate for her deodorant, a toothbrush, and some scented lotion.

Why had she never actually gotten around to making the emergency refresher kit she had thought about so many times?

Maybe Ryker would take her to a drugstore really quick . . .

He opened the door to the steakhouse, gesturing for her. "After you, milady."

She inclined her head very regally and marched by him. "Thank you, sir."

Ryker snorted, then came to her side, draping his arm across her shoulders. "Ah, it's good to see you, Bree. I miss you."

Bree smiled and leaned her head on him as best as she

could while walking, slipping her arm around him and patting his back. "I miss you too, dork. Season's over; you could come see me more."

He glanced down at her. "With my wife's shooting schedule?"

"Are you a wealthy professional athlete married to a Hollywood actress, or aren't you?" she demanded without shame.

"Point taken." He pulled her in closer and kissed the top of her head before ruffling her hair. "I'll figure something out."

Bree shoved away from him, biting back an almost curse word her roommate was particularly fond of as she ran her hands down her hair to smooth it, flicking the miraculously still-curled ends a little to bounce them. The one time she actually did something to her hair, and she had spent hours in a crowded arena sweating with thousands of others despite the cold. Her hair was probably frizzed to the point of what-do-you-call-that-hairstyle by now.

"Hair's nice," Ryker commented at just the wrong time. "You do something to it recently?"

Scowling at him, Bree collected her hair in one hand and draped it over her left shoulder, away from him. "I *did* my hair. That's what it is."

He held up his hands in defense. "Okay, sorry, just asking."

She made a face and walked ahead of him into the back room they'd reserved.

"BREE!" came a wall of sound as she entered, startling her.

"Oh my gosh, seriously?" She looked around at the group of them, shaking her head. "I literally just saw all of you. Why would you do that?"

"It's just so much fun!" Sawyer explained, coming over to give her a quick hug. "You have the best name for cheers."

Bree raised a dubious brow. "You need to get out more. Before Erica pops."

He shrugged happily, his impending fatherhood seemingly not terrifying him. "What do you call this trip?"

"I have no idea." She moved away from him to Rachel, who wore a similar expression of longsuffering tolerance.

"Hi," Rachel sighed, looking as tired as Bree felt.

"Save me," Bree groaned, pulling out a chair and sinking into it. "Why do we get dragged into these things?"

"Because we're their family and they love us," Rachel recited, just as someone had inevitably said every time that question had been asked. "Diet Coke?"

Bree nodded emphatically. "Please."

Rachel picked one up from a nearby tray on a tall table. "I ordered some ahead. Preemptive strike."

"Bless you."

They shared similar smiles while the Six Pack proceeded to behave like hyper teenage boys.

Typical.

"How did you marry one of them?" Bree asked when Cole suddenly howled like a coyote.

Rachel sighed. "To be fair, I didn't marry that one."

"Points to you, but still."

"Eh. Grizz is hot, and I fell for it." She pulled out the chair next to Bree and sat down. "How's life? We didn't get to talk at the game."

Bree shrugged, making a quick face. "Fine. School and stuff, but I'm almost done. Clint coming to town is a highlight."

She bit her lip hard at admitting that. Rachel might be a

friend and a fellow Six Pack Sib, but she was also Clint's sister-in-law, of all things.

If Rachel suspected anything by that, she gave no indication. "Clint's great that way," she admitted to Bree, smiling softly. "Really good about putting people at ease. Might be a McCarthy trait, actually. David's amazing at it, and the others . . . I don't know, his parents are that way . . . "

"You're that way . . . " Bree broke in, her tone taking on the same list-like note Rachel's had.

The addition earned Bree a quick smile. "Thanks, babe. Maybe it comes with marriage." She leaned back, her eyes widening as she looked at Bree. "You know, Chicago's a quick train ride, if you need a weekend away."

"That's not a bad idea," Bree murmured, considering the idea.

Then she remembered.

"Well, like I said," she added hastily, "Clint being in town helps. Gives me something to do outside of school."

"Oh yeah? Like what?"

Oh crap.

"CLINT!"

Bree turned to the front of the room as the guys cheered in welcome. Clint walked in with his parents, grinning and raising a hand to slap high fives with everyone. His hair was damp, his black T-shirt perfectly fitted, and the cut on his cheek wasn't bleeding, even if it was visible. It was already starting to bruise, but it gave him an almost-dangerous look. An edge.

Something virile.

She swallowed harshly. "Did the kids go back to the hotel?" she asked Rachel with as much innocence as she could manage.

"Yeah, it's too late for them." Rachel grinned quickly. "Emily and Eric were pretty mad, but they're the oldest, so..."

"And will Uncle Clint or Uncle Grizz be making it up to them?"

"Probably. They usually do." Rachel rolled her eyes, though her smile was warm and affectionate.

"Okay," Clint said over the noise of the others, "can we eat? I'm starving."

"Get the man a steak!" Axel bellowed playfully.

"A raw one," Levi suggested, leaning back in the chair he sat in. "For his shiner."

The room reacted in varying degrees of appreciation, but for Bree's part, it wasn't very much. Attractively dangerous edge or not, that hit to the face had scared the life out of her. Seeing the cut now made her wince just as much as it made her strangely proud.

Clint gave Levi a dark look. "Your lady give you that tip, Steal? She's the tough one, I hear."

Cole whooped loudly at the comeback. "Shots fired! I got fifty bucks on Fido!"

"A hundred," Grizz and Sawyer said at the same time.

"Come on," Rachel groaned at her husband and her brother, not bothering to distinguish between which one annoyed her most.

Levi only grinned, which was one of the rarest sights in existence, and shrugged. "So what if she is? I'm man enough to admit it."

"Ten points to Levi," Bree said without thinking.

All eyes moved to her in an instant.

Levi beamed at her. "I love you, kid."

"Great," Bree replied, her cheeks coloring at the sudden attention. "You can buy me dessert."

"Happy to."

"Wait, wait, wait," Ryker interrupted, waving a finger in the air. "We compliment our ladies, and you get dessert out of the deal? When was this arranged?"

"Sit down, Rabbit," Grizz groaned as he sat beside Rachel, resting his arm on the back of her chair. "If you ask really nicely, someone might compliment you, and then Bree can support it, and maybe she'll share second dessert."

It was the most perfect thing Grizz could have said, and suddenly everyone was complimenting each other ridiculously, nobody remembering Bree's part in it, so the attention was removed from her.

Her cheeks were still hot, and she put a hand to one, silently breathing to try to cool them down.

She glanced down the table to find Clint staring at her, not talking to anyone at all and smiling very softly.

Fire started down at her toes, but her lips didn't seem to know that as they smiled back at him.

Which made his smile grow.

Which made the fire worse.

She grabbed for the Diet Coke on the table ahead of her, her fingers slipping on the condensation at first, then, with another almost curse, she snatched the glass and sipped through the straw deeply. Gulping down the carbonation without tasting or thinking, she looked over the menu, trying to ignore how her chest hurt for the full course of that swallow.

Stupid carbonation.

Everything she read blurred together as one in her mind as she wondered if Clint was still watching her. This was nuts; she wasn't this nervous to see him any other time. They'd been ridiculously comfortable together, and she hadn't felt the need to pretend anything or put on a show.

She didn't need to have it all together for Clint.

Until now, anyway.

Her fingers drummed against the hard plastic cover of the menu, looking up as the server entered, her stomach rumbling. "Chicken tenders with honey mustard, side of mac and cheese, and can I also get a side salad with ranch?" she recited when asked.

"Yes, ma'am."

Bree exhaled as he moved on, glancing at Rachel. "Apparently I'm eight years old in my dietary preferences."

Rachel shrugged. "I got a BLT and fries. No judgment here."

This was why she loved Rachel. Kind of hated her for the kind of body she could rock while eating whatever she wanted, but when one considered the hours of work Rachel put in as a professional dancer, it seemed fair enough.

"Clint," Grizz suddenly called down the table. "What's eating Zamboni? You guys get into it earlier?"

Bree's attention flicked down to Clint, whose smile faded.

"It's been a few years, Grizz," Clint replied without emotions. "People change."

There was a definite note of finality in his words, and no one could miss it. He didn't want to talk about the hit or the guy who had delivered it.

Why? If they knew each other, why wouldn't he talk about it? That would have been something fun, a photo op, at least.

But that hit had been anything but fun.

It had been ugly.

And the table felt it.

Clint wasn't looking at anyone anymore, just down at his knuckles, and it made Bree want to hug him for some unknown reason.

"How did it feel, Clint?" she asked, her voice tight with other questions she would much rather ask.

His eyes raised to hers, almost wary.

She let herself smile, her hands clasping together between her knees. "Being out on the ice tonight. Your first game as a Hawk."

His slow smile curled the ends of her hair and the walls of her stomach. His eyes never moved off of hers, and they might have been alone in someone's living room.

She wished they were.

"Amazing," he said softly, and for a second, she forgot what she had asked him. "It felt amazing."

Yeah. Yeah, it did.

A slow exhale escaped her, almost a sigh, her smile gentling. It had felt amazing to be there, to watch him, to know him off of the ice after seeing him on it.

The whole thing had felt amazing.

Still did.

"On a scale from zero to riding the Scrambler after three corn dogs," Cole began in an almost-serious tone, "how close to upchucking were you before the faceoff?"

The room erupted with laughter and groans, and Clint's smile turned into a full-on grin as his attention moved to Cole. "Why do you think I skated around the rink so many times? Nice cool breeze settles the stomach."

"That must be why Axe Man takes so many practice swings before he bats," Ryker mused aloud with a sage nod. "Nerves. Gets him every time."

"Hey!"

Bree laughed with the rest of the group as they all settled in for the meal, individual conversations taking place now instead of a mass one. She preferred it like this.

"Bree."

She looked over at Clint's mom in surprise. "Mrs. McCarthy?"

She smiled indulgently. "You can call me Aubrey, sweetie."

There was no way she could do that, but Bree smiled anyway. "Okay."

Mrs. McCarthy's smile spread. "We're going to be in town as often as we can for Clint's games, and we would love to take you out whenever you're free."

"Oh, you don't have to!" Bree shook her head. "This is time for you guys. I don't need to . . ."

"Of course we do," Mr. McCarthy interrupted in his almost-booming-but-always-cheerful voice. "You're practically family."

She absolutely was not, especially when she couldn't keep her eyes off of Clint for more than five seconds at a time.

As if it was inevitable, she looked at him again.

That same soft, satisfied smile was on his lips as he watched her, hearing every word.

She had no response for the sweet offer from his parents, especially since she wanted, more than anything, to spend more time with Clint. But with his parents too?

That felt huge somehow.

She bit her lip, her brow wrinkling with a question she couldn't ask aloud.

Clint's mouth quirked more on one side than another, and his shoulders lifted in an almost-imperceptible shrug.

Then, to her shock, he nodded.

An immediate smile spread across Bree's face, her heart leaping into the craziest jig she'd ever felt. "I'd like that," Bree told the McCarthys, her eyes staying on their youngest son. "I'd like that a lot."

Clint's smile grew, and that stupid idea of climbing across the table to kiss him returned.

It wasn't that stupid this time.

It wasn't stupid at all.

"Hey, Fido," Sawyer suddenly asked loudly, "how do we get one of your jerseys to wear around? Need to get mine before the price gets jacked up with your popularity."

"Just ask," Clint said simply, blatantly staring at Bree now. "Just ask."

Bree swallowed hard. She raised a brow, the question there.

Clint didn't react at first, then, of all things, he winked.

The Hawks might have lost the game that night, but Bree Stone had just scored.

And the crowd went wild.

EIGHT

"Why do we like this sport?"

"Because it gives us great bodies."

"Not you."

"Whatever."

"No, seriously, why?"

Fig looked at Clint in disbelief as they sat against the wall, their legs shaking against the force of it and the weights on their thighs. "Because it's the greatest sport on earth, that's why. Now shut up. I'm not doing more line drills than we have to."

Clint chuckled breathlessly, leaning his head back against the wall with a grunt. Coach was in a mood today, so their conditioning had been brutal. Circuit days were nobody's favorite, and while he'd started out doing great, this fourth time around might actually kill him.

He'd rather do drills for hours on end than conditioning. Not that the Marines hadn't given him plenty of experience in pushing his body past what he thought it could tolerate, but he'd always prefer being on the ice to anything else.

That never got old.

Never would.

"You shakin', Fido?"

Clint groaned in agony as their strength-and-conditioning coach, aptly named Coach Payne, came over to the row of them in the same group currently enduring wall sits.

Coach Payne squatted down and smiled in Clint's face as he laid another twenty-five-pound plate in Clint's lap. "You're a Marine, Fido. Marines don't shake. Marines don't quit. Marines do not show weakness."

"No, sir!" Clint barked out of sheer habit, something stiffening in his spine despite the pain from his waist down.

"If I asked you to run three miles now, would you run three miles?"

"Yes, sir!"

"If I asked you to sit here for another hour holding those plates, would you sit here and hold those plates?"

"Yes, sir!"

"No pain."

"No pain!"

"No fear."

"No fear!"

"You weak, Fido?"

"No, sir!"

"At ease."

Clint exhaled roughly and sagged to the floor, the rest of his group doing the same.

Coach Payne grinned down at him. "Semper fi, McCarthy."

Panting, his entire body trembling with fatigue, Clint nodded, his lungs screaming for air.

"Two tours myself, son," Coach Payne told him, straightening and putting his hands on his hips. "Nothing like the heart of a Marine."

Clint grinned in spite of his exhaustion. "Tell that to my legs, Coach."

Coach Payne chuckled and blew his whistle, waving the other groups in. When they all arrived, sharing in their same level of pain, exhaustion, and misery, the coach cleared his throat. "All right, one easy lap around the concourse, then that's it. Get yourself cooled down, get your treatments in, and report back here tomorrow at oh nine hundred. We're off to Denver right after practice for the Chargers, so pack well. Hook, what's the dress code this time?"

Hook, dripping with sweat, wiped his brow. "Men in black. Suit it up, fellas. It'll look great for our media team."

Good-natured chuckles went around the group.

"Hawks on three," Hook called. "One, two, three!"

"HAWKS."

Clint shook his head to himself, amused by the raspy quality of their cheer today. Pain did interesting things to the voice.

The team moved as one to the concourse, jogging lightly on already-quivering legs.

"Feel better, Fido?" Fig asked as he and Junior joined him in the run.

"Like a million bucks," he shot back. "Love me a good workout."

"Uh-huh." Junior rolled his eyes, though his shirt was damper than either of theirs. "What a rush."

They really didn't say much after that, words and speaking too draining after their workouts while still running.

Clint didn't mind; the run felt good for his legs. Made them a little less angry about earlier and kept him from going completely stiff. A good soak in an ice bath after this and another easy run in the evening, and he'd wake up good as new for tomorrow.

Amazing how he'd settled into a routine so quickly. Of course, with their intense playing schedule, there wasn't much else to do but acclimate, and he'd done his best to do so. There had been three games since his first, and all of them away from St. Louis. Now they were about to head to Denver tomorrow, but just for the night. Three home games in a row after that, and he was grateful for it.

He needed to spend some time with Bree.

As usual, he smiled at the thought of her.

That was something else he'd settled into quickly. And easily. And intensely.

It was crazy: they'd been talking every day, either texting or calling, even when he was away, and it still wasn't enough. He missed being with her when he was away, despite it only being two weeks since they'd started seeing each other.

Two weeks.

Well, more like two and a half.

Big difference.

He'd defended it in his head time and time again; they'd known each other for years, after all. Quick and intense could be considered normal under the circumstances. They hadn't been close over the years, but what did that have to do with anything?

They were close now.

But what were they?

Two weeks, and he wanted a definition?

Ridiculous.

"Enjoy the moment, McCarthy," he muttered to himself.

There was no need to rush anything. After all, that was the best part of being with Bree; she was so comfortable and refreshing to be around. Their conversations hadn't gone anywhere particularly serious, and there hadn't been any need for them to. There wasn't a checklist of things to discuss while they were together or while he was out of town; they only had to be together.

Even silence was comfortable with Bree.

He tended to be more silent than she was, remarkably enough, but that was because he usually caught himself staring instead of speaking. Every time he saw her, it was like he couldn't believe he really was seeing her. Such a gorgeous, natural-looking woman without airs or effort, and addicting to be around.

He'd never forget the dinner after his first game. A room full of people, and his eyes kept coming back to her. What had struck him was that her eyes seemed to do the same to him. So many smiles, so many unspoken messages, so much to feel . . .

If they'd had a single moment of privacy that night, he'd have kissed her.

That thought had startled him, but he hadn't been able to get rid of it since then.

The urge to kiss her had faded somewhat, so he wasn't constantly on edge, but he had noticed himself looking for opportunities. That was a terrifying threshold, though, and he wanted to make sure he wanted to cross it.

He wanted to make sure *she* wanted to cross it.

Bree was special, and he wasn't the kind of guy to throw physical intimacy into a relationship right away. Maybe he was old-fashioned in that regard, but he'd never minded that title much.

She didn't seem to mind either.

He jogged to a stop as he reached the stairs towards the locker room, following his teammates down. Bree would be in the library on campus for most of the day, but he could probably convince her to sneak away for dinner, at least.

Or maybe ice cream.

She seemed to have a weakness for ice cream, and he had no shame in exploiting that if he needed to.

He laughed to himself as he moved to his locker, digging into his bag for his phone to text her.

There was already a message waiting for him, but he didn't recognize the number.

Interesting...

He opened it, more than a little curious.

Hey boys. Jax Emerson here. Been a minute, hasn't it? Listen, you're going to be getting an email from the Northbrook chairman of the board, Deacon White, in a day or two, and I'm gonna need you to take it seriously. The club's in trouble, and I think we owe it to them to check it out. Easy for me to say—I'm home in Chicago—but they've checked all our playing schedules, so they know we're free. Might just be this one time, so do what you can to get here. For Hal, if for no other reason.

Clint stared at the screen of his phone, reading the message at least two more times before he could look away.

Jax Emerson. He hadn't seen him in at least eight years, if not more. One of the better players Northbrook had ever seen, and they had seen a fair few.

The club was in trouble? Northbrook was one of the select elite hockey clubs in the country; how could it be in trouble? There had been community support, sponsors, and scholarships for the talented kids who couldn't afford the fees, and it was one of the best hockey training locations in the world. The camps every year alone had a waiting list that rivaled some universities. Clint had been fortunate enough to play for the feeder program as a kid, and he was convinced that was the only way he had made it to the elite squad.

There was no way Northbrook was in trouble.

But Jax... Jax wouldn't be involved if something wasn't up, and he definitely wouldn't reach out to Clint if it wasn't serious.

He checked the phone again and counted four other numbers in the group message.

None of them were saved as contacts.

Which of his former teammates would be included?

Or were they guys from before or after his time? There were plenty of guys to choose from before his time. Northbrook had a long history of talent. After his time was a little different, mostly because Clint had stopped paying attention while he was in the military full-time.

Bitterness can make you do strange things.

He wasn't bitter now, of course. He'd fought his way up the professional-hockey ladder by the skin of his teeth and his own willpower. But being one of the only guys from the team not drafted had never sat well with Clint, so he'd walked away.

Or so he'd thought at the time.

Maybe that was unforgivable to the guys.

Maybe that was what had earned him such an insane hit from Zamboni.

He could see that, actually.

His phone buzzed in his hand, and he looked down at it.

Zamboni in, bros.

Great.

Of all the guys he didn't need to see off of the ice again, Zane was probably at the top of the list. Nice enough guy, bit of a knucklehead, great player, but a complete animal once his skates hit the ice. Complete transformation that terrified those who didn't know what to expect.

He lived, breathed, and died for hockey; he'd have a hard time forgiving Clint for leaving, for sure.

Plus there was his stupid use of the word *bros*, as though he had been raised on a surfboard, drinking suntan lotion in the '90s. That was a new trait, given that he was as Chicago-bred as they came.

Score one for against the trip home.

The Rock is in, man.

Clint hissed at the new message.

Rocco was a good one. All heart, wore his emotions on his sleeve, and had the most wicked slapshot Clint had ever seen.

That was a definite tally in the Go category.

This was ridiculous. He had just gotten to St. Louis with his team and was settling in before the season really took off. There was no way he could ask for a day off of practice and just head up to Chicago in the middle of all of that to check on his old club. He'd basically severed ties years ago.

He might be back to playing hockey now, since the love of the sport had never died, but it wasn't the same thing.

Couldn't be.

After a quick shower and change of clothes, he headed out of the Hawk facilities and jumped in his car without much by way of conversation with his teammates.

He didn't need them right now.

He needed Bree.

His phone buzzed again before he got on the road, and he quickly checked his messages, the strangest sensation of anxiety hitting him squarely in the chest.

I'll try. —Dice

Dang, Jax was pulling out all the stops if he was going for Dice. Declan Rivera played for Denver, which meant Clint would see him tomorrow.

His eyes widened as he thought of that.

Dice was an incredible defender on the ice. Not as much of a bruiser as Zamboni, but more than capable of cleaning up when the situation called for it.

Was Clint in for a penalty-inducing injury from him, too?

His still-tender cheek twinged at the thought.

Exhaling through his nose, Clint pulled out of the

parking lot and headed towards Bree's campus. He punched the Bluetooth button and said her name.

If she was in the library, she wouldn't pick up, but he could send her a text if the call went to voicemail.

"Hey," her voice suddenly answered, the throaty tone of it making him smile in spite of his fairly tumultuous train of thought at the moment.

He loved that her voice was as natural as her personality, that it wasn't high-pitched or bubbly or grating. It was a voice you wanted to listen to. A voice that soothed.

A voice to crave.

He cleared his throat. "I thought you were at the library."

"Eh, I gave up," she said, the sound of wind accompanying her.

"You walking on campus?"

"Yeah, just headed back home. Why, you need something?"

"Just you."

There was silence on the other end, and Clint held his breath, waiting for her response, wondering if he'd pushed too far with his quip.

"Okay," she said slowly, but he could hear her smile. "Where do I need to be for you?"

A grin flashed across his face. "Wherever you are is good enough for me."

Bree laughed once. "Not really. I'm in the middle of the square, and you'd have a tough time getting here from any of the parking lots. You coming from practice?"

"Uh-huh."

"'Kay. Smith and Keystone lot is easiest. There's a great place to sit, if you want."

"Sitting with you would be perfect." He swallowed as he said it, the fervency catching him off-guard.

"You okay?" Bree immediately asked. "What's wrong?"

Clint shook his head, even though she couldn't see him. "Nothing's wrong."

He heard her rushed exhale. "What's not right, then? Something's up. Don't pretend it isn't."

She was good; he'd give her that. Reading him easily without even seeing his face. Either that meant something or he was a terrible actor.

Maybe both.

"I'll tell you more when I see you," he said, turning off the interstate, "but I might need to go to Chicago next week."

"And why do we sound reluctant for a trip home?"

Now it was his turn to exhale in a rush, the tone of it eerily similar to hers. "Because it's a trip to see Northbrook and some of the guys, not to see home and family."

"Uh-huh. Remind me, babe, who's Northbrook?"

Whatever he was going to say caught in his throat with a painful lurch. Did she just call him . . . ?

It could have been raining, snowing, or hailing, and he would have said it was the most glorious day the world had ever seen. If he were not currently going fifty miles an hour, he'd pull over and do his best imitation of a touchdown-celebration dance out in the middle of whatever road he was on.

He'd never wanted to kiss her more in his entire life than right now.

"Clint?"

Right. Conversation.

Babe.

His face flushed. "Northbrook," he answered quickly. "The hockey team I played for in junior high and high school. I guess the club is having some trouble."

"Okay, so . . . ?"

"I haven't been back in years. Haven't seen any of them in years," he admitted with more pain than he'd expected. "I mean, you remember Zamboni from the Nashville game?"

He heard her dark laugh. "Not likely to forget that piece of trash and his dirty hit, am I?"

Clint bit back a laugh of his own. "He was on that team with me. He's already committed to going."

There was no sound from her end for a moment, and then just a very small, "Oh."

"Uh-huh." He waited a moment, then shook his head. "Honestly, I don't know if I want to go after that. I basically walked away. What if they're all going to be like that?"

"What if they all intentionally crash you into the wall and make you bleed?"

He smiled at that. "They're called boards, Bree."

"Whatever. I doubt that's going to happen. You're going to let that guy and his roughing the passer keep you from reconnecting?"

Now he was laughing. "Just roughing, Bree. No passer."

"You know what I mean. It was just a hit, right?"

"It was personal."

"You don't know that."

He hummed knowingly. "Kind of do."

"So be bigger than the hit. The Clint McCarthy I know isn't worried about if everybody will like him. He holds his head up high, works hard, and keeps being the same good guy he's always been. People tend to like him anyway when he's himself."

He grunted in satisfaction. "Do they?"

"Yep. I do, at least."

Her words sank into him like rays of the sun, and he was momentarily unable to speak.

He liked her too. A lot more than he had ever expected to.

"Did I lose you?" she asked when he didn't respond.

"No," he assured her, his throat aching with the word. "No, you didn't lose me."

"Good."

Suddenly he had the feeling they weren't talking about cell phone service, but he couldn't be sure.

Wanted to be sure.

He slowed the car as the parking lot neared, and he pulled in, a familiar brunette sitting with her ankles crossed on a raised cement planter. She'd braided her hair loosely over one shoulder, and her fleece jacket was only half zipped. She waved at him and stowed her phone in the pocket of her jacket, her legs swinging just a little.

Comfortable, beautiful, warm, natural Bree . . .

He loved the very sight of her.

Smiling, he got out of his car and headed directly for her. "Hello, beautiful."

She gave him a cheeky grin and hopped down from her seat. "Hiya." She looked up at him as he neared her, her eyes searching his. "You okay?"

Clint nodded as he reached for a long strand of hair dancing in the fall breeze. "Yeah," he murmured, twisting it behind her ear. "I'm okay."

Bree leaned into his touch, then slipped her arms around his waist and hugged herself to him, nestling her face against his shoulder without any hesitation whatsoever. "Good."

His arms instantly wrapped around her, cradling her, and he wished he could somehow pull her into himself, carry her with him wherever he went so he would never lose the feeling of having her right here. He laid his head atop hers, letting himself sigh as he held her. "Yeah," he said again. "This is good."

Her arms tightened around him further still in response.

NINE

SHE'D BITTEN HER nails down to almost-painful stubs.

Trista would be horrified. She'd completely understand, but she'd be horrified.

There wasn't anything Bree could do about that now. Ever since she'd said goodbye to Clint yesterday morning before he'd left for Denver, her nerves had shot up to an all-time high.

Well, maybe not all-time, given the number of times Ryker had been injured over the course of his career, one of which had actually scared her to the point of tears, but she was certainly anxious enough now. She had barely eaten breakfast this morning, lunch had been laughable, and Penny had physically taken away her phone to stop her from incessantly texting Clint.

Now that they were only a few minutes from the start of the game, Bree had her phone back.

Mostly for emergencies.

But would anybody know to contact Bree in the case of an emergency?

They'd call the McCarthys, not her. As they should, for sure, but would the McCarthys call her?

Her fingers flew along the keypad of her phone, Grizz's number popping into the contact line.

"No," she muttered to herself, forcing her fingers to stop. She exhaled long and slow three times. "No." She deleted her frantic message quickly before shoving her phone in the pocket of her hoodie.

Clint's hoodie.

It was stupid, but he'd left it in her car the other day, and she hadn't exactly gotten around to giving it back.

She might never.

It was large, it was warm, and it smelled like him. At a moment like this, that was all she could want. Short of having him here with her, this was perfect.

As calm as she had been when he'd first brought up going to Chicago and seeing the guys from Northbrook, her mind had spun since then. He'd opened up eventually, after he'd simply held her for ages, and he had given her the rundown of each of the guys he had been closest to. It had been an interesting conversation; she could hear the note of regret in his voice, and the almost longing tone when he spoke of their time as a team.

And then to know that Zane had hit him like that? On purpose?

Clint didn't have a good explanation for it.

And now he was playing another former teammate. He'd assured Bree that Dice—Declan—was very different, but it didn't make her feel any better.

She kept having visions of even more brutal hits that would end with Clint lying unmoving on the ice like the end of a particularly horrible boxing match. She suspected that was a touch dramatic on her end, but as her experience with hockey was limited to that first game with Clint, she really didn't know what to expect. He'd come away unscathed from his games since then, it was true, but he hasn't been playing old teammates with a potential grudge.

Why would anyone hold a grudge against Clint? What could he have done?

Bree swallowed hard, her fingers lacing and twisting with each other over and over. Had anybody ever died from an injury in hockey?

"Whoop!" Penny dashed into the room, decked out in black and purple Hawks gear. "Game time! Game time! Let's go, Hawks!" She looked at Bree with a bright, vivacious grin. "You ready for this?"

No, she wasn't, but she forced a smile anyway. "Absolutely!"

The microwave dinged, and Penny ran over to it. "Popcorn's done! Want a drink?"

Bree nodded, but knew she wouldn't drink much of whatever it was. She stared at the TV in apprehension, waiting for the commercials to end, knowing the game would be on next.

"All right," Penny said as she brought the bowl of popcorn and some drinks over. "I'll order some chicken wings for the second period, but this should tide us over for now. Here you go."

Taking the chilled can, Bree managed another smile. "Thanks, Pen."

Penny eyed her, then shook her head. "Where is your team spirit, Breezy? Turn around."

Bree did as she was told and felt her hair being pulled back into a ponytail. "What are you doing?"

"I did not grow up a Hawks fan for nothing," came the huffed response. "My sister and I made these hair ties for a fundraiser when we were kids, and to this day I have dozens. The least you can do is wear one."

The ponytail was pulled right, and Bree pulled out her phone to check her reflection in the camera. Strips of purple and black fabric stuck out at odd angles from the band, and if she tilted her head down enough, she could see a plastic hawk fastened to the center of it.

Clint would have a field day if he saw this.

"Perfect!" Bree said with a laugh, grinning up at her roommate.

"I know." Penny folded her arms, her expression smug. The theme song for the sports network blared from the TV, the camera panning around the inside of the Denver arena—a sea of green and white, their fans clearly as passionate as the Hawks fans had been at home.

Bree exhaled slowly as she saw players skating on the ice in warmup, wondering which was Clint. The camera wasn't close enough to see jersey numbers, so she could only guess.

Please don't get hurt . . . Please don't get hurt . . .

"Amy!" Penny bellowed, making Bree jump. "Get out here! Our boyfriend is on!"

"Your what?" Bree asked with a laugh.

"Boyfriend," Amy repeated as she hurried out of her bedroom and into the living room. "Oh good, you made snacks."

Bree looked between her roommates in bewilderment as Amy took a fistful of popcorn. "Who's your boyfriend, and why are you sharing him?"

"Clint," they said together.

Now she was totally lost. "Excuse me?"

Amy gestured for Penny to explain as she tossed some popcorn in her mouth and situated herself on the couch.

"Apartment boyfriend," Penny told her without concern. "We concede that he is your particular boyfriend, but as Amy and I are currently unencumbered by any such attachment, we claim him as ours when it suits us. It's a status thing."

"I see," Bree murmured, her lips forming an affectionate smile for these two, even if their antics were a little ridiculous. "Does Clint know this?"

Amy shook her head firmly. "Nope, but we'll tell him next time he comes over. We're the family-and-friends-package candidates, so we should have reserved seating at games. Apartment boyfriend gets a fan club if he goes along."

It was one of the silliest things she'd ever heard of, but she would let it go, especially since it made her less nervous for the moment.

There was one thing that she ought to clarify, however.

"He's not my boyfriend."

Her roommates gave her the exact same deadpan expression. "Uh-huh," they said together, their tone disbelieving.

"He's not!" she insisted. "We've never . . . said that."

Amy waved her hand dismissively. "Technicality. That boy is yours, babe. Lucky. Ooh, I do like me a goalie . . . "

Bree bit her lip as she returned her attention to the TV, the announcers saying something about the Hawks' goalie, John Cheswick.

"Is he single, Bree?"

"No idea," she replied with a smile. "I don't know any of them."

Penny grunted in thought just once. "Consider this your next assignment, then. Get to know them."

"Noted."

She wouldn't mind finding out the details of Clint's teammates and their relationship status. It would be a small price to pay for being with him.

She would love to get to know the team. To be more involved with them. To be part of something.

With him.

They might not have definitions yet, but she would be his

girlfriend if he asked. She already considered herself his . . . something.

Whatever this something was.

But was he hers?

She knew full well what went on among some pro athletes when they traveled, and a lot of the time when they were at home. Ryker might have protected her from the nitty-gritty details, but she was no fool. Rules and regulations for a team were flimsy at best, depending on the coach and team culture. *Frat boys with athletic ability*, she'd once heard her brother call them.

Clint wasn't that kind of guy, but that didn't mean he'd feel particularly attached to her. He could go out with the guys, meet some gorgeous woman who'd fit on the arm of a professional-hockey player, and get splashed across the headlines of magazines, tabloids, and websites. It would fit with his life now.

Quiet, naïve, plain, unimpressive Bree Stone wouldn't fit. She'd just finish her education, start her career, and let the people who belonged in the spotlight stay there.

No need to make a fuss.

Why should she bother?

The announcers' voices faded on the TV, and she focused on the screen, her heart pounding as she realized that Clint was right there.

Front and center.

Exhale . . .

The puck was dropped, and it shot over to Hotch, who raced forward with it. A green player was immediately on him, his stick reaching out to interfere with his. The puck moved in Clint's direction, but a green player got to it first and started towards the center of the ice.

Bree tried to follow the play as best as she could, reacting a few milliseconds behind Penny's outbursts, usually in the same vein, as Penny clearly knew more about the sport. For the most part, she followed well enough, but the constant switch of players in and out of the boxes while play was going on made zero sense. Whistles were blown at random times, and she couldn't understand why for the most part.

Someone would need to walk her through this sport at some point if she ever wanted to get anywhere.

Clint could not be with someone so ignorant of the sport that was his life.

"Who'd you say he knows on the Denver team?" Penny asked, sitting on the edge of the couch and clapping about something in the game.

Bree cleared her throat, making herself focus on the present, not insecure what-ifs parading in the way of enjoying Clint's game. "Dice. Declan something."

Amy hummed in satisfaction. "Declan Rivera. Right there." She pointed at the screen, to a defender currently scuffling over the puck with one of Clint's teammates on the boards. "Can I cheer for him?"

"No," Penny and Bree said as one.

"Pity."

Clint was suddenly back in the game, somehow clambering over the box and racing down the ice with Fig and Hotch, the pair of them moving to their respective sides. Clint seemed to fly between three of the Denver players, almost like a pinball in a machine, darting back and forth as he tracked the puck. Hotch and Fig closed in, but they had their own Denver players to contend with.

The puck suddenly shot forward, past Clint and the others, and Bree gasped loudly, her hands clenching into fists. But one of the Hawks' defenders scooped it up in his stick, sliding it from side to side before firing it back towards the opposite goal.

Fig took it, raced forward, then, for whatever reason, sent it soaring around the rink behind the opposite goal.

"Why?" Bree yelled, her hands flying out with the question.

"Wrapping it is fine," Penny assured her without looking. "See? Hotch is there. Watch out!"

Hotch, who had gotten to the puck first, now had two players basically blocking him in.

"Get it out!" Penny bellowed.

On command, the puck moved out of Hotch's control and was easily scooped up by one of the Hawk defenders, who moved it towards center ice, and Clint.

Clint weaved one way, then the other, then dropped it towards the other defender.

What was this? Why take it back into their own territory?

A lone green player followed the puck, hovering close to center ice, watching the defenders, who shot it between each other once, twice . . .

Then the puck shot forward again, directly to Fig, who sped towards the goal, crossing the puck to Clint, flying up on his right.

"Go, go!" Bree urged, her fists flying to her chin.

Clint suddenly veered to the far right, away from the goal and defenders, Hotch coming up behind him.

A Denver player was hot on Clint's heels, though, and suddenly slammed him into the boards, Clint's stick flying out of his hands even as the puck moved to Hotch.

"No!" Bree yelped as Clint went down on the ice.

A whistle blew as the puck suddenly went screeching past the goal without going in.

Bree didn't care. She kept her eyes on Clint.

The defender who hit him was back, a hand on Clint's pads, hoisting him to his feet. The guy said something to him, and Clint grinned, of all things, before his helmet was ruffled almost like his hair would have been.

Bree found herself smiling as Clint jokingly elbowed the guy, taking his stick back from one of his own players. He was blood free and still smiling, and he said something over his shoulder.

Relief washed over Bree, and she sat back hard against the couch.

"Huh," Penny said as the players all lined up for another faceoff. "Maybe we can cheer for Dice."

"That was Dice?" Bree looked at the screen hard, thinking back as play resumed.

"Uh, yeah." Amy snorted loudly, munching on more popcorn. "Told ya. I like that guy."

"We can't like him while we're cheering for our boyfriend," Penny reminded her. "Any other team, fine, just not ours."

"Okay, I guess . . . Ooh, nice save, my next boyfriend!"

Bree rolled her eyes but settled in for the rest of the game. If Dice wasn't going to target Clint the way Zane had, she could relax a little. The outcome of this one game wouldn't change anything, and Clint was an amazing player, so he could handle himself.

She smiled slightly as he returned to the box, even if the camera continued on the play at hand and the new line freshly in. The puck moved so quickly back and forth on the ice, and the players so freely from end to end at any given moment, that it was hard to keep track of which team was better and if either team outplayed the other.

What made a good game or a bad game? Outcomes helped, she was sure, and if he scored a goal, it was probably a good day, but when goals weren't being scored, how would she know?

These were the sort of questions she would need to ask him if she actually wanted to be his girlfriend. She had experienced her brother's moods after games, whether good or bad, and had always tried to modify her behavior accordingly. Usually she knew what to expect based on the game.

But that was baseball.

She knew baseball.

What about hockey?

"Hey, Penny," she suddenly said, sitting up again, her eyes on the screen. "I need your help with something."

"Now?" Penny groaned. She gestured at the TV. "Our boyfriend is on. *Your* boyfriend is on. We've got enough to do."

Bree grinned at that, remarkably not even blushing. "I know that. This is for our boyfriend."

That perked both of her roommates up. They looked at each other, then at her. "Yes?"

Bree glanced at the TV, biting down on her lip with sudden excitement. "I need you to teach me hockey."

Amy belted one loud laugh, and Penny's brow furrowed with apology. "Oh, sweetie. I don't play."

Now Bree laughed. "I don't want to play hockey. I want to *understand* hockey." She gestured to the game, where a fight was breaking out, thankfully not involving Clint. "I was raised on baseball. I don't understand anything here, and for Clint, I need to know."

Penny beamed, a distinct twinkle of mischief in her eyes. "Yes, you do, Breezy girl. Yes, you certainly do." She patted the seat next to her. "Scoot over, sunshine. Amy, order us some chicken wings. Tutoring session has commenced."

TEN

THIS WAS SO weird.

He had only ever entered this building with his bag slung over his shoulder and a bagel in his hand, so walking up this particular sidewalk empty-handed was the strangest sensation he'd known in some time.

Clint shook his head, shoving his hands into the pockets of his leather jacket, wishing he had listened to himself and just forgotten this whole thing. Why did he need to reconnect with old teammates and touch base with his hockey roots anyway?

As he glanced up at the building, two things registered: the building looked exactly the same, and it looked horrible.

It had needed upgrades when he left, and the last he knew, those upgrades had been forthcoming. The only thing he could tell was even remotely different was that the place had aged. It showed more wear and tear, less cleaning, less landscaping, and absolutely no upkeep.

A few kids raced by him, their hockey bags as big as they were, and they darted up the stairs ahead of him. He smiled at that, wondering if they were excited, apprehensive, or both.

He had only been late to a practice or two in his entire life, and there was no forgetting that fear. Coach Hal Fenwick, legend that he was, expected and demanded the very best a player had to offer, and the commitment to go with it. Late arrivals paid for their infractions with the dreaded Tardy Drills, and even the workouts he endured today paled in comparison.

Emotionally, anyway.

Physically, it was different. The work he put in now was by far more intense, but during those Tardy Drills, you knew death was imminent.

"Respect our time," Coach Hal would say, "and we'll respect yours. Respect the sport, and it will respect you. Respect your teammates, and they will respect you. Respect yourself, and the rest of the world will too. Respect is given, and respect is earned. Give it, and earn it."

Respect. Maybe that was the driving force keeping his feet moving towards this building full of memories.

The ice of this place had shaped him into the player he was today; the lessons of this place had made him into the man he was.

He exhaled slowly as he reached the top of the steps, his hand going to the bar of the door.

No turning back now.

With a yank, the door swung open, and Clint was hit with a wall of memories. The smell, the sounds, the annoying buzzing of the lights overhead, and the edge of frost to the air that reminded you ice was near. Home away from home back then, and just as familiar to him now.

Who'd have thought?

He followed the main hallway, past the glass cases with team trophies and photos, and took the first flight of stairs up to the boardrooms. He could hear the whistles of coaches in the distance and the sound of blades against ice, and he suddenly had the feeling that he would much rather go there than where he was headed now. He was a hockey player first and foremost, and he'd much rather battle out whatever was coming out there than up here.

He knew how rough the ice could be; he had no idea what to expect from this.

"Here goes nothing," he muttered to himself as he hesitated outside of the boardroom, then turned the handle and pushed the door open.

Four guys sat around a huge table, and they all looked at him when he entered.

"Well, well, well," the biggest one said, turning in his chair, black baseball cap backwards on his head, drumming his fingers on the wood of the table. "If it isn't Mr. Semper Fi himself."

The coolness in the tone was unmistakable, but there wasn't anything to be done about that now.

Clint nodded once. "Zane."

A corner of Zane's mouth lifted, and he startled Clint by pushing up to his feet and extending a hand. "Should have started with this the other day in St. Louis."

Blinking, Clint took his hand, shaking it hard. "Good to see you."

"Good to be seen." Zane grinned in his usual way. "My biggest fear, you know. Not being seen."

"Mmm, pretty sure everybody sees you coming." Clint dropped the handshake, sliding his hands back into his coat. "Except for me in St. Louis."

Zane showed zero remorse, but there was also zero anger. "That was a good one."

Clint shook his head, unable to keep from laughing to himself. Zane hadn't changed a bit. "I wondered if it was a sign of affection."

"Nah." Zane shook his head, shrugging. "Just knew I could get in a good hit without someone thinking it was personal."

"I *did* think it was personal."

"Yeah, I just felt like hitting you."

Clint raised a brow at him. "And the elbow?"

"Okay, that was personal."

"Why?"

Zane folded his arms, his upper-arm tattoo of a sabercat, the mascot of Northbrook, peeking out from the sleeve of his T-shirt. "You don't write, you don't call . . . "

Clint scoffed a laugh. "Neither do you."

"Let's not focus on me right now."

"Give it a rest, Zamboni," another voice called out from the table. "Let the man come in, at least."

Zane grinned and turned around, returning to his seat. "You know what, Diesel? I'm tired of your opinions."

"Tough, man."

Clint managed a weak sigh of relief as he removed his jacket and took a seat at the table, nodding in greeting at the intimidating guy giving Zane a hard time. Trane "Diesel" Jones was one of the toughest people Clint had ever met, let alone played with. Came from a rough part of the city, grew up just as rough. But turned it all around with just a few years in the Northbrook programs. Now he was one of the slickest goalies in the league, as well as one of the most feared and respected.

"Sup, Fido?" he greeted with a small smile. "You look good, man."

"Thanks." Clint glanced over at Dice, who gestured a salute with two fingers. They'd just played in Denver and had caught up a little then, so he didn't feel the need to talk much.

That had been a huge relief. Dice's reaction to seeing him

had given him the final nudge he'd needed to make the trip to Chicago. If Zane wasn't going to line him up for another hit, maybe this whole thing would be worth it.

"Since when did you get a new name, man?" Rocco asked from his chair, rocking back and forth like it sat on some porch in the country. "You stop liking McTrouble?"

Clint smiled at the reminder. "You're the only person who ever called me that, you know."

"Shoulda stuck with it." Rocco shook his head in disappointment. "Could have been famous."

"Fido's a pretty good name," Trane pointed out. "Plus he's a Marine. It works."

"I didn't say it didn't work, I just said the other one was better."

"No, it wasn't," the other three said as one.

Rocco threw his hands up. "Where's Jax? He'll back me up."

The door opened just at that time, and it was clear that Jax had caught the end of Rocco's statement. "Not likely. No offense, Rocco."

A chuckle went around the table, and Clint turned to greet Jax, who looked a little too serious for his liking but nodded at Clint anyway.

Jax was followed into the room by a middle-aged man with a receding hairline in a suit. The guy was built like a hockey player, but he was clearly a has-been at this point. His smile at the gathering was tight and did nothing to make Clint feel better.

"Hey, boys," Jax said, standing at the head of the table, his thumbs hooking into the pockets of his jeans. "Thanks for coming out. I know we're all busy, but this is important." He gestured to the man in the suit. "This is Deacon White, chairman of the board here. He wants a word."

And just like that, Jax sat down in the nearest chair, his attention immediately going to Mr. White.

What was going on here?

Mr. White moved to the head of the table. "Gentlemen. Thanks for showing up. I knew if we got Jax here to send the message out, we'd get a better response than if I did it myself. I'm a Northbrook alum myself, played here in the '90s. Not quite as good as you all—I never went pro—but some of my best memories are in there on that ice." He jerked his thumb over his shoulder in the direction of the rink.

Clint found himself nodding, more inclined to listen to someone who not only knew the sport but knew Northbrook.

"Jax told you that I am chairman of the board here," Mr. White went on with a sigh. "The truth of the matter is . . . I am the board."

Clint blinked hard, positive he'd heard the man wrong.

Rocco's incessant rocking stopped. "Say what?"

Mr. White nodded. "There is no board of directors at Northbrook anymore. There's just me."

Jax sat forward, his eyes narrowing. "Since when? There used to be all kinds of positions on this board. What happened?"

"Maybe seven years ago, a couple of major businesses that had been supporting us couldn't afford to donate anymore." Mr. White shrugged. "Then some other local companies opted out. After that, we had to increase fees to keep up the cash flow, and that didn't go over well. Parents didn't want to pay, the scholarship program couldn't be supported, and numbers started going down. When numbers went, so did interest."

Clint raised his hand, his brow furrowing.

"Mr. McCarthy," Mr. White invited, pointing at him.

"I think, out of us here"—he paused to look around at the

table—"I'm the most recent Northbrook alum. When I left, all of the talk was about the new facility. I remember my parents talking about it, the plans were approved, and the funding was in place . . . "

Mr. White nodded along with everything Clint was saying, his expression never changing. "We were in negotiations for final details of all of that when we started losing our funding. Money had to be diverted towards things we needed most. Equipment for the kids, travel expenses, tournament fees, scholarships . . . " He offered a helpless shrug. "Northbrook is dying. We don't even have a full squad in the elite program anymore. Camps are a joke, the feeder programs just trickle in. We have people who only come because, and I quote, 'there isn't anything better to do,' so you can imagine what *that* does for our reputation. There's no money for advertising, and clearly there's no money for upkeep. We're bleeding out, fellas. The only people on staff here anymore are Coach Hal Fenwick and me."

That took a moment to sink in, and Clint, for one, slumped back hard against his seat.

How had such a dominant and popular program gone so far downhill so fast? The waiting list for even the feeder programs had been insane growing up, and it sounded like there wasn't even a need for one now. The team parents of Northbrook had been incredible, and the board always fully staffed with capable, intelligent people who were invested in the programs and in the community. He couldn't even count all of the fundraisers, service projects, community outreach, and a dozen other things they had done as a team and as a program.

All of that was gone now?

"Coach Fenwick is still around?" Trane asked with a slight smile. "That's something."

Mr. White did not return the smile. "Fenwick wants to retire. He's been doing this for forty years now, and he's tired."

"So why doesn't he?" Dice gestured for emphasis, a furrow deep in his brow. "There has always been a team of assistant coaches here. Surely someone would be happy to come take over."

"A dying program with no money?" Mr. White shook his head. "Believe me, Declan, I've put out more feelers than I'd care to admit. No one is interested in taking over Northbrook as is. And if Fenwick goes now, the program will die out with him. And that's not an exaggeration. I've asked about that too."

No one had a response to that. The clock on the wall ticked in perfect time, each second seeming to be an agonizing reminder of what they had just been told.

Northbrook couldn't go under. The cases down in the hall held relics from teams past that had won their divisions, even gone on to national championships. If they were to track it down, Clint was sure the number of former Northbrook players who had gone into the pros would be astounding.

The two kids he'd seen racing into the building suddenly returned to his mind. Did they have the passion for hockey that every kid who'd skated on that ice in earlier years had? Or were they some of the newer ones who'd only come because there was nothing else to do?

"So what do you need from us?" Jax asked slowly. "Money? A news spot?"

For the first time since he'd entered the room, Mr. White looked as old as he must actually be. "Honestly, I don't know at this point. All I know is we need help, and you six are probably in the best position to help me figure out what we can do."

Clint stared, wide-eyed, then looked around at the others

and found similar expressions of near shock and an almost windswept look. He didn't know about the others, but he wasn't exactly rolling in massive amounts of money. He'd only just been called up; his contract wasn't even worth fighting over yet. He *couldn't* fight over it yet.

He had nothing to offer in the efforts to save Northbrook.

"Okay," Zane said slowly, sitting forward to rest his elbows on the table. "Let's brainstorm."

An hour later, and no good ideas had come from them. Creative ideas, sure, but nothing actually feasible. It was one of the most discouraging meetings Clint had ever had to sit in, and he'd made it a point to avoid the type of work and life where meetings, other than team ones, were a necessity.

Silently, the six players and Mr. White filed out of the boardroom.

"Well, if you guys think of anything, let me know," Mr. White said with a tired smile. "I know it's a lot to take in. Email, call, text, whatever, if you think of anything or need more information."

They all made some sort of farewell grumble as he waved and walked away from them, leaving the group standing there.

"Well, that sucked," Zane said, leaning back against the wall.

Dice shook his head. "I never thought the club would tank like this. It was always a beast, you know?"

"I wouldn't be a hockey player at all if it weren't for this place," Trane admitted bluntly as he looked around. "Never could have afforded this without scholarships. If not for Northbrook, I'd straight up be in jail for sure."

"I didn't know he meant that kind of trouble," Jax murmured, looking almost lost. "I thought they might need us to give the club a boost or something, not actually save the place."

Rocco grunted. "Think Daddy Money can buy the team out, Golden Boy?"

"Rock..." Dice warned, shaking his head.

Jax didn't rise to the bait, Clint was relieved to see. "I won't pretend it hasn't crossed my mind, but even if he did, he'd put himself on the board, and that wouldn't help anybody." He ran a hand over his hair. "Even if we had the kind of money to save the place, it's not like it would keep things sustainable."

"Sounds real smart, Jax," Zane interjected from the wall. "Almost sounds like you went to college."

"Clint went," Dice pointed out.

All eyes turned to Clint.

He held up his hands in surrender. "Uh, I did two years of juco to rehab my knee and keep in shape, and that is all that can be said for my educational background."

Zane thumped his head against the wall three times. "Well, I got nothing, but I don't really think off the ice. You boys wanna skate?"

They all perked up at the suggestion. "Is the ice free?" Rocco asked eagerly.

"Who cares?" Zane shot back. "We're the big time, and we're alum. I say we just do it."

Nobody had any better ideas or particularly strong objections, so they walked over to the stands of the rink, watching the last few skaters finish up drills.

It was nostalgic and tragic at the same time. The kids were laughing and teasing each other, calling out encouragement and heckles just like they used to do. The drills were just as familiar to Clint now as they had ever been then, and in fact, they'd done a more advanced version of this drill in practice just the other day.

The tragic part was seeing the kids themselves. Not one

of them had the sort of hockey gear they ought to have training with Northbrook. There had once been a standard set of equipment that each player received when they joined, and as the players grew, new ones were ordered. There had been practice jerseys in the traditional green or white of the team, always fairly clean and in good conditions, but these kids were playing in faded, torn, falling-apart jerseys.

They could have even been the same ones Clint and the others had worn when they had been their age.

This wasn't Northbrook; this was something else entirely.

But the love of hockey was there. He could see it in each of the kids' faces. Coach Hal wasn't even on the ice; it was a few of the older boys running these drills for the younger kids.

"Boy, does that take me back," Dice said to no one in particular.

Nods rippled around the group, then Zane gestured for them all to follow him down the stairs to the locker rooms, though any of them could have led. It was a path they could have done in their sleep, and probably had done for some of their early morning practices.

They each picked up a pair of skates from the stockroom, though none of them were particularly high quality, and headed out to the rink, the kids from the ice passing them on their way in. No one paid them any attention, none of them were recognized, and it wasn't until they got out to the ice itself, where the older kids were picking up equipment, that a word was even said.

"Hey," Zane called to one of them, gesturing as he skated. "You mind if we borrow a few sticks and a puck?"

The teen's eyes went wide as he looked up at Zane, obviously recognizing him. "You're . . . you're . . ."

"Just an old Sabercat looking for some practice," Zane finished with a grin. "That okay with you?"

"Yeah." The teen nodded and handed Zane the stick in his hand. "You can use mine."

Zane hefted it in his hands as if weighing it. "That's a nice one. Good job, kid. What's your name?"

"Tyler."

"Awesome. Tyler, I'm going to use this to play with my crew, then I'll sign this for you and leave it in your locker. What's your number?"

"Seventeen."

Zane groaned. "Aww, man. Dicey! The kid's in your old locker, dude!"

Clint shook his head as they all skated over to the teens, picking out their sticks and making small talk for a few minutes.

"Do you . . . want us to wait around?" the other kid asked, looking at Jax in confusion. "To get the lights and lock up? Coach Hal left us in charge."

Jax put a hand on the kid's shoulder. "Nah, we've got this. Trust me, we've had to lock up a time or two in this place, and that isn't something you forget."

The teens nodded and skated off the ice, looking over their shoulders and talking softly to each other as they did so.

Clint chuckled and looked at his former teammates. "You enjoy doing that, don't you?"

Zane shrugged without any concern whatsoever. "One of the perks. I like being a big deal. Now come on, Fido, let's see what kind of skills they taught you in the Marines." He gave Clint a playful shrug before skating over to the far side of the rink, pointedly icing the net. "Hey, Diesel! Come sit in your pocket!"

"How I haven't managed to kill that knucklehead yet is

beyond me," Trane muttered as he followed at a more leisurely pace, tapping the hockey stick against the ice rhythmically as he went.

"This feels so weird," Jax murmured to Clint as they moved to center ice.

Clint nodded his agreement. "So what are we going to do about the club?"

"No idea."

Rocco came over to them, joining in the conversation. "Did you see their jerseys? Cheap quality and well used. Didn't we get new ones every year?"

"At least every other, for sure." Clint exhaled slowly. "We've gotta figure something out, though. This place can't go under."

"Absolutely not."

"Hey!" Zane yelled from his zone. "Are we going to play, or are we going to talk about it? Come on, I got things to do before I get old and gray!"

Jax grinned reluctantly and nudged Clint in the shoulder. "Still remember how to do Humpty Dumpty?"

Clint laughed once and nodded, digging his blades into the ice a bit. "Oh yeah. Might be out of practice, but I got it."

"Excellent ... " Rocco bobbed his head to some silent beat in his head, smiling at them both. "Zamboni hated that one. I bet he can't stop it now any more than he could stop it then."

"Dice might catch on," Clint warned, eyeing the other defender. "He's smarter."

"Nah." Jax shook his head and started for his spot to the left. "I got Dice. Let's show 'em what the Power Line still has."

Now Clint threw his head back, laughing effortlessly and without any hesitation. "Were we really that pumped up about ourselves?"

"Were?" Rocco gave him a superior look. "I still am. Come on, Fido, hit 'em hard."

Clint looked down the ice, a feeling of satisfaction washing over him. He looked around the seats of the rink, once filled with family and friends, all fans decked out in green and white, screaming at the top of their lungs. Echoes of that same energy lived in the rafters, and if he listened, he could hear the Sabercat fans with their chants.

Dang, he'd loved this place.

"Fido?"

Clint glanced over at Rocco, giving him a crooked grin. "Ready?"

The Italian grinned back and lowered himself into faceoff position. "Ready."

He looked at Jax, who was already set, and nodded with a wide smile of his own.

"Come on, chickens, the defense is snoring over here!"

Clint lowered himself into the set position, his eyes fixed on Zane as the guy practically bounced on his feet. He exhaled softly, his grin never wavering.

Payback was going to be a glorious thing.

ELEVEN

"Oh my gosh, this is so much better than on TV!"

Bree laughed and looked at Penny and Amy, standing beside her as they cheered for the beginning of the third period of the Hawks game. "How's that? We can't see them as well up here."

"But the sounds, Bree!" Penny gushed, spreading her hands out. "The energy!"

Well, Penny wasn't wrong, but that wasn't exactly what Bree wanted from coming to Clint's game.

He'd just gotten back from Chicago last night, he was playing in this game now, and she hadn't been able to do more than talk with him on the phone while they'd been apart.

Today she'd had class all day, and she had never been more tempted to completely skip class in her entire life.

Three days. That was the entire length of time they had been apart. The most time they'd been apart since they had started seeing each other, and she'd felt like she needed to claw her way out of her own skin that entire time.

She still felt a bit of an itch and burn in her palms and the tops of her feet.

The only way to get rid of it, she knew, was to see Clint. To be with Clint.

To define something with Clint.

What, she didn't know.

But it was definitely something.

She watched as Clint slipped over the edge of the box, racing out into the game with two other guys, strangely not Fig and Hotch tonight, and found herself cheering a little louder, her heart racing within her.

He looked so powerful on that ice, so fast and so skilled. His endurance had to be incredible, given how often he went from end to end over the course of his shift.

Bree smiled and nodded in pleasure. Penny had been quizzing her the past few days, bringing up other hockey games on TV to help explain her point, not to mention some online. She still didn't quite understand all of the penalties, but at least her terminology was correct.

It was a start.

And a start was better than nothing.

"Come on, come on, come on . . . " she hissed as Clint went flying up the ice, weaving around other players, the puck flying from his stick to his teammates' and back again with a dizzying speed.

Someone took a shot on the goal, but the goalie caught it easily and dropped it around the back of the net to one of his own teammates, who sent it up the ice to safety, forcing Clint and his line to race back.

Bree glanced up at the scoreboard, where the numbers read a tied score at two points apiece.

"SLASH!" Penny suddenly bellowed with the rest of the enraged crowd.

"What did I miss?" Bree asked, trying to figure out what had happened and why play hadn't stopped when it did.

Penny sputtered in irritation, gesturing to the ice. "Twenty-three over there decides to hook Farraday like he's being yanked off a stage while Farraday is making a press, and the blind ref doesn't think it's a slash!"

Bree stared at her roommate, then looked further at Amy, who was smiling in reluctant amusement. "It's like she's trying to speak English, isn't it?"

"Kinda, yeah."

Penny grumbled and waved it off. "Never mind. Suffice it to say, that should have been a foul. Stick to arm, no bueno."

"Got it." Bree returned her attention to the ice, where Clint and his line were hopping back into the team box and a fresh line, clearly fired up by the bad call, flew into action.

The puck went this way and that, more like a pinball in a machine than anything she'd seen yet, and she could barely keep up with it. One of the Hawks suddenly sent it around the boards behind the goal, only for another Hawk player to pick it up, dart forward, and . . .

"GOAL!" Bree, Penny, and Amy shouted at the same time the buzzer sounded.

The crowd around them erupted with them, chanting for the Hawks, banners, towels, and team jerseys waving above heads while certain sections jumped up and down in the stands like a student section at a college basketball game.

Clint and the others in the box were on their feet cheering, banging their hands against the walls of the box, thumping their sticks on the floor beneath them.

Bree, for one, felt herself breathing just a little bit easier.

She wouldn't mind seeing Clint no matter what the circumstances, but after how she had been feeling, she would much rather have it be after a win.

On the other hand, he might need some consolation after a loss . . .

Her face flamed, and she took the opportunity to sit down, fanning her face.

"You okay, Bree?"

She nodded at Penny's question and smiled up at her for effect. "Overheated. Lots of people and energy . . . "

Penny nodded sagely, and maybe with a little pity. "Water bottle under the seat. Have at it."

Bree nodded and started chugging it, dripped a little on her fingers, and ran those fingers behind her ears and across her brow.

It didn't do much, but at least she felt better.

Distraction. All she needed was some distraction.

"Heyoo, there's our boyfriend!"

Bree sprang up, burning face and all, almost gasping in her enthusiasm, which was borderline ridiculous as far as reactions went. She was at Clint's game. She had seen Clint play before. None of this was new.

It didn't matter. She had to watch, had to see, to make sure he played well, didn't get hurt . . . What if he did something spectacular? What if something horrible happened?

She'd never felt so drawn to watching anything in her life.

Great, now she was obsessed.

Low point.

But watching him, seeing him in action, didn't feel like a low point. She was thrilled watching him. Being here and knowing how she felt about him while watching him do something he loved and was so good at . . .

Wait, how did she feel about him?

How did one describe a compulsion towards obsession with one she still imagined randomly crossing a table and kissing?

Bree blinked and shook away the deep thoughts that gave her anxiety.

Clint was on the ice, and her focus needed to be there too.

"Come on, babe," she murmured as he scuffled with another player against the boards, fighting over the puck.

When had she started calling him babe anyway? She'd never called anyone any sort of endearments in her life, apart from calling her brother all sorts of things. This was some new and random instinct, but she liked it.

Really liked it.

Clint broke free, the puck now with his teammate, and then, suddenly, it was back to him. He seemed to just flick the end of his stick, firing the puck towards the goal. The goalie reached for it, but the puck sailed into the top-right corner of the net, out of reach.

The arena let loose with an explosion of sound, and so did the Hawks' box, whooping for Clint as he punched gloves with his teammates on the ice, grinning.

"Way to go, Fido!" Penny bellowed before putting her fingers to her mouth and ripping a shrill whistle that blended perfectly with the other sounds of the place.

Bree could only smile and applaud, her cheeks aching from smiling, the warmth in her face now in the center of her chest and spreading to the tips of her fingers.

Clint was amazing.

And it felt amazing to like him as much as she did.

He needed to know that.

The rest of the game, what was left of it, was uneventful, and the crowd, as diehard as it had been, started to thin out before the final buzzer, now that their team was ahead by two. Sure enough, when the clock ran out, the score was still four to two.

Penny and Amy left after a few minutes, telling Bree to congratulate their boyfriend for them, and they gave her eerily identical smiles of mischief that embarrassed her to no end.

She really needed to get over that.

Slowly, she made her way back up to the concourse, her jacket over one arm, slinging her crossbody bag over one shoulder. She had a pretty good idea where the players came out, since some of them signed autographs after games, so she headed in that direction.

Maybe she should text him . . . It was entirely possible he had already made plans for after the game with some of his teammates, or that he would just want to go sleep. He had been traveling, after all, and had just finished an intense game.

He might not want to see her.

That seemed unlikely, even to her, and Clint would never say that, but in a completely impersonal way, he might just want to be alone and go home.

Crap, what if he didn't want her to wait for him?

And when had she become such an insecure mess?

Feeling more than a little ashamed of herself, Bree lifted her chin and continued down to the players' exit, opting to stand out of the way of the fans wanting autographs but still in perfect view of the door. The players would have to come by her to get to their cars, so it would allow her to gauge the situation as needed.

If nothing else, she could wave and give him a thumbs-up before heading out alone. They were friends, so why shouldn't that be allowed?

Something was better than nothing, she reminded herself.

Or would nothing be less painful?

The door to the team rooms opened, and Bree watched as a few players she didn't know came out, some of them signing autographs, others just waving. One or two took the time to take pictures with whoever wanted them, much to the amusement of the security guys hanging around. It was clear they were used to this scene, and for some reason that made Bree happy.

Ryker and the rest of the Six Pack had always made an effort for fans—thought it was really important to give them time—and the public loved them for it.

This was something to be proud of.

Bree smiled as a familiar face came around the barrier towards the parking lot, right in her direction.

"Well, hi there, Miss Stone!"

"Hey, Mario. Good game."

Mario shrugged nonchalantly. "It was all right. Pulled out the win, so that's fine. Looking for Fido?"

Bree blushed a little. "Is it that obvious?"

The tall Canadian grinned at her. "Well, nobody would assume you were here for me, pet. Hang tight." He leaned closer to whisper, "Don't tell him I said so, but Fido isn't the fastest person out of the showers. Not the slowest, but definitely not the fastest."

"I'll keep that in mind." Bree laughed as she relaxed against the wall behind her. "I'm not in a hurry."

"That's good, cuz you won't be hurrying any time soon." He winked and waved, walking past her out to the parking lot.

She wouldn't mind waiting around for Clint, however long it would take. Ryker was painfully slow in getting ready, always had been, and she'd grown up just dealing with that. After games, it was even worse. She'd always joked that Ryker was more high-maintenance than she was, but as they'd gotten older, it had become less and less of a joke.

Just a fact of life.

That was fine—she didn't care. And if Clint didn't feel like hurrying, that was also fine.

A few other players came out, most of whom she didn't know, and then, finally, there was Clint.

He didn't see her at first, but he was getting a decent amount of attention. New to the team or not, Clint McCarthy was making his mark, and the fans were noticing.

Bree watched as he signed autographs, took a few pictures, and talked to some kids at the barriers. He was so good with them, smiling and taking the time to engage with each one brave enough to talk with him.

For someone who didn't want much by way of attention, he sure did a good job in handling it.

After taking one last picture, Clint smiled and waved at the fans, then headed in her direction, his head down.

At this rate, he'd walk right past her without any idea she was there and had been waiting.

He looked up and stopped, staring at her for a moment, his expression as close to stunned as she'd ever seen him look.

"Hey," she said softly, straightening up and slipping her hands into the back pockets of her jeans. Nerves all over her body began to tingle in anticipation, a blend of good and bad. She shifted her weight to try and release some of the tension coiling in the pit of her stomach, but all it did was flare it up more.

It was ridiculous how good he looked this close.

"You're here," Clint finally said, his mouth curving into a crooked smile.

Bree exhaled a gust of relief and smiled back. "Yep. I'm here."

Clint's bag was dropped, and he marched over to her, shaking his head. "It is insane how much I missed you."

Her feet were moving before she meant for them to be, and she found herself jumping into his open arms, pulling him close and thrilling at how clenched Clint's hold around her was.

This is perfect.

"Why does it feel like you were gone forever?" Bree asked, burying her face into Clint's shoulder.

"I don't know," he growled. He exhaled into her hair, which she had left down that day and might never put up again if he kept this up. "I don't know, but I didn't realize how hard that was until I saw you just now."

Bree hummed a laugh and let herself be lowered down, but she stayed close to Clint, linking her hands behind his neck. "You were so great tonight. That play in the second period was amazing, and when you and Fig teamed up to get the defender in the boards? So good."

Clint chuckled and touched his brow to Bree's, cupping her cheek with one hand. "Look who's picked up some hockey lingo."

She punched him lightly in the stomach. "Hey, it's not my fault I'm from a baseball family. I'm trying here."

"I know you are," he assured her, still laughing. "And it's ridiculously cute. Means a lot, Bree."

She smiled, sighing a little. "I figured if I'm going to hang around here more, I should probably figure out what's going on. Penny and Amy have been teaching me, and when we got our tickets tonight . . . "

"Wait, wait . . . " Clint pulled back and gave her a look, his hands going to her waist. "You guys bought your tickets?"

"Yeah . . . " Bree laughed at his expression. "Why, were we not supposed to?"

He shook his head, grinning. "From now on, your name will be on a list at Will Call. I get four seats a game, and if my parents aren't in town, they are all yours."

"And if they are in town?"

Clint brought his brow to hers again, his steel-blue eyes holding her hazel ones captive. "You always have a ticket. You hear me? Always."

Her heart was going to cartwheel out of her chest and break into a dance routine somewhere behind her, she was sure of it.

She wet her lips carefully, forcing herself not to grin like an idiot. "So you want me to hang around, huh?"

He grunted softly and brought his lips to press a kiss against her brow. "Yeah, Bree," he murmured, his lips warm against her skin. "I want you to hang around."

Inhale... Exhale... Inhale... Exhale...

"Okay," she whispered, the grin taking over anyway. "Okay."

Her lips began to buzz, and her knees began to shake. She wanted to arch up and kiss him, wrap herself up in him, do something about the aching need constantly gnawing at her whenever he was around. Her pulse pounded, and she could feel Clint's breathing growing as uneven as hers was.

"Bree..."

Yes...

"Hey, Fido!"

Bree could have growled at whoever was interrupting this moment. Couldn't they see this was not something to get in the way of?

Clint exhaled roughly and turned to whoever it was, keeping his arm around Bree's waist. "Chezzy?"

A broad-chested ginger-haired guy with a big grin was heading towards them, and Bree had the sense this guy knew exactly what was going on there. He had chosen to break it up and was getting a kick out of this.

Jerk.

But there was no arguing with that smile, and for all Bree's scowling, she found herself managing a small smile for the newcomer.

"Wanna get some food?" Chezzy asked in all-apparent

innocence, adjusting the strap on his shoulder. He looked at Bree, and the smile turned more mischievous. "Hi. John Cheswick."

Bree nodded once. "Bree Stone. Nice to meet you."

"Same." Chezzy returned his attention to Clint expectantly. "You in?"

Clint shook his head, still smiling. "No thanks, man. I've got plans tonight."

Chezzy did not seem at all surprised and shrugged. "Too bad. Maybe next time." He smiled at Bree and raised two fingers in a sort of wave. "Have a good night, Bree."

"You too, John," she said back, bemused by this guy who reminded her so much of the Six Pack.

Clint dropped his arm from Bree's waist and returned to his bag, picking it up and coming back to her, gesturing for the parking lot. "You ready?"

She nodded, slipping her jacket on. "So," she said after a moment, "you have plans? What are they?"

"Whatever you want," Clint told her without hesitation. "I don't care. I just want to be with you."

Be still, her pathetic heart.

She smirked in his direction. "I don't have any plans either."

Clint slipped his hand into hers and laced their fingers together as though it was the most natural thing in the world. "Well, let's get out of here for step one."

She held his hand tightly, rubbing her thumb against his skin. "Good idea. Step two?"

"Don't rush me. I'm working on it."

"Sorry."

They walked in companionable silence towards his car, Bree, for one, unable to stop smiling.

"Did you really not know that hockey is played in

periods?" Clint suddenly asked, his tone full of unshed laughter.

"Hey!" she protested. "Not a hockey family, not hockey fans. I've only been ice skating maybe once in my life, okay?"

"What?" He shook his head in dismay. "If it weren't so late, I'd take you to a rink right now. This is not okay."

"Neither is keeping a girl waiting after a game, but . . ."

"I didn't know you were here! You gotta text a guy these things."

"Next time you'll know, right?"

"Next time I'm running from the ice right to you, no excuses."

Bree leaned against him, hugging his arm to her with her free hand. "Sweet thought, but a shower is okay. I saw you after the game, and that was a lot of sweat."

Clint chuckled and kissed the top of her head. "Can't have it both ways, babe. Either I'm fast, or I'm clean and I smell good. Pick and choose."

She inhaled the scent of him pointedly, then sighed. "Smelling good is fantastic. Let's go with that."

"You got it. You come to the game, I'll come out of it smelling however you want."

"Deal."

TWELVE

His phone would not stop buzzing, and it was getting really annoying.

It was funny—hilarious, even—but annoying.

It was probably making up for lost time, but Clint had never thought that the Northbrook guys were all that chatty.

In the last few days, they could have passed for a pack of high school girls. The moment one of them sent a selfie doing the stupid duck-lips pout, he was blocking all of them. Every single one.

Which one would take that selfie?

Clint thought about that as he drove towards Bree's apartment, the idea giving him more enjoyment than it should.

Zane, he decided. It would absolutely be Zane.

When he reached a stoplight, he pulled his phone out of the cupholder and looked at it.

"The Pit?" he said out loud, looking at the new name at the top of the group text. "What in the world?"

He scrolled back through the messages to figure out where that had come from.

Jax: Sup, guys. CRAZY workout today. Can't feel my legs.
Zane: And we care ... why???
Jax: You'll care when we own you guys next month, Zamboni.
Zane: Bring it, Flyboy.
Trane: This is cute.
Dice: Barf.
Rocco: Don't take this the wrong way, but I might start sharing pics of my food if this keeps up.
Zane: So help me, Rock, if you turn this group text into a preteen Snapchat...
Rocco: Ha, just because you eat mac and cheese four days a week and can't boil water.
Jax: Since when do you cook, Rock?
Rocco: ... I'm Italian, idiot.
Trane: NO WAY. Why didn't you tell us?
Dice: In all seriousness, Rock, if you have recipes that are less than twelve steps, I'll take them. Always looking for good food.
Zane: I'm pretending you didn't say anything that reminds me of my stepmother's recipe group.
Jax: Haha, we could call this group Your Mom's Recipes.
Zane: No.
Trane: Why are we naming it?
Rocco: Makes the group easier to find on your phone. Duh.
Dice: If this group is named anything, it better be totally masculine. I'm not associating with something I can't admit to in public.
This group's name has changed to The Pit.
Rocco: Who did that?
Zane: What the ... What does that even mean?
Trane: Means you need deodorant, bro.

FACEOFF

A honk broke Clint out of his almost hysterical laughter reading over his texts, and he looked up to see a green light. He waved an apologetic hand to the car behind him and drove through the intersection, replacing the phone on the seat beside him.

Ever since that game on the ice with his old teammates, they'd stayed in contact on an almost-daily basis. Some were more talkative than others, but they were all involved. Sometimes they shared stupid things, sometimes comments about each other's games, sometimes randomly pitching ideas for the club. There wasn't much they'd settled on, but it wasn't for lack of trying.

Clint, for one, was strapped for ideas. He'd spent a full hour on the phone with his brothers just the night before in a complete brainstorm session. As they all lived in the Chicago area, they promised to look into some local options and get back to him. Grizz had offered to talk to some of his teammates on the Flames, but Clint wasn't sure they needed to do that quite yet. Jax was in Chicago, too, after all, and the hockey team might be in a better position to help a hockey club.

Grizz was adamant that the specific sport didn't matter; Clint agreed but wanted to give Jax the opportunity first.

He hadn't really told Jax the idea of using his team, the Flyers, to help the club, but surely that would occur to him.

If worse came to worst, he could always ask Cole Hunter from the Six Pack. Cole had a fortune independent of his baseball earnings, and a good investment in an athletic program that was once so involved in the community might intrigue him.

But again, reaching out to the Six Pack, as close as they were, as much as he respected them, seemed a little needy.

Desperate.

Mooching.

Clint wrinkled up his nose as he pulled into Bree's parking lot. Surely there was a way for the group to figure this out without asking their friends for money.

Like Jax had said before, just having the money wouldn't sustain the program.

So what would?

Shaking his head, Clint climbed out of his car and walked up the path to Bree's apartment, forcing his worries over the program into the background. Tonight was about Bree and him, and he was going to make it special. He needed to make sure Bree knew that *she* was special to him, that she was important to him, and that he was invested in them.

In her.

In wherever this led.

There was no point in fighting this attraction to her, this need to be with her; it was as natural as the air he breathed and twice as refreshing. He'd never been in a relationship like this, and he wondered how anybody who had experienced it ever wanted anything else.

He couldn't imagine wanting anything else.

Anyone else.

"Bree!" a voice within the apartment hollered before he'd even knocked on the door. "Our boyfriend is here!"

Clint raised a brow at that, smiling to himself. Since when had he become community property?

The door swung open, and Penny stood there in her sweats and oversized T-shirt, copper hair slung over one shoulder in a loose ponytail. "Hi, Clint."

"Penny," he said with a nod. "How's the term project?"

She rolled her eyes and stepped back, gesturing for him to come in. "Public relations would be a fantastic field if it didn't have so many people in it."

He laughed once, then actually started nodding as he

thought about it. "I get that. People make everything more complicated."

"Amen." She shook her head and moved to the couch, her laptop on the coffee table. "It'll be fine once this week is over. What I wouldn't give for something I can actually sink my teeth into. This is just boring." She heaved a sigh and put her head in her hands for a second, then looked up at him with a smile. "What's on the docket for date night, Captain Blue Eyes?"

Clint gave her a bemused look. "Captain Blue Eyes?" he repeated. "That's a new one."

"Marine plus attractive feature equals nickname," Penny elaborated quickly. "Tell me what you're doing tonight."

"Can't do that, I'm afraid. Top secret."

Penny groaned. "A hint, at least. You're killing me."

Clint glanced towards the bedrooms, then lowered his voice. "You had lesson one for her. Terminology. I have lesson two, hands-on."

Her eyes widened. "You mean . . . " She lifted a socked foot and mimicked lacing skates.

He nodded once and held a finger to his lips.

She mimed zipping her lips and gave him two thumbs up with a huge grin.

"Thanks." He exhaled heavily, looking towards the bedrooms again.

"Bree!" Penny bellowed, making him jump. "Don't keep the poor man waiting!"

"Penny Marquette, leave me alone!" Bree barked in response as she came out into the living room, smiling as she widened her eyes in exasperation. "It takes some effort to look this good."

Penny scoffed loudly and waved a hand. "Effort, schmeffort. You're a natural, and I hate you."

"I love you too," Bree replied, batting her eyelashes. She looked at Clint with a warm smile that made his chest ache. "Ready?"

"Yep," he managed, holding out his hand. She took it at once, and he looked back at Penny. "See you, Penny."

She nodded. "Captain. Have fun, you two."

Bree shook her head as Clint led her out of the apartment, sighing once the door was closed. "I can't believe she called you captain."

"Oh, she explained the whole thing," Clint told her as they walked to his car. "But what I want to know is when I became 'our' boyfriend."

Bree's gasp was flat-out comical. "You heard that?"

"Oh yeah." He gave her a cheeky grin as he opened the passenger door for her. "Loud and clear."

Her cheeks went rosy in the chilly evening air, and she clamped down on her lips hard. "I have no explanation for that."

Clint shrugged as she slid into her seat. "Fair enough, but I'm really only interested in being one person's boyfriend." He gave her a pointed look as he closed the door.

Bree's eyes widened, and she looked forward almost immediately.

Chuckling, Clint moved around to the driver's side door, opening it and climbing into the seat. He debated continuing the conversation but opted to simply start the car and back out as though the point had been made well enough.

After all, he'd said his piece, and there was an entire evening ahead of them.

It was entirely possible there would be a solid answer by the end of the night.

Bree was silent on the drive, and Clint wondered if he had said too much, pushed too far. He rested his hand between their seats on the console, watching out of his peripheral vision to see how she would react, holding his breath.

Three heartbeats passed, and then Bree reached over and took his hand, pulling it over to her side, weaving their fingers together before placing her free hand on top of them.

Slowly, Clint released his breath through his nose, glancing over to see Bree staring out of her window. But her hands were on his, and her hold was sure.

That was enough.

"Where are we going?" Bree eventually asked. "I can honestly say I have no idea where we are."

Clint laughed once. "No? Good. I've been taking the long way to throw you off."

She slapped his hand sharply. "Clint! Come on, that's just mean!"

"It is not! It's sneaky. Excuse me for trying to surprise you." He grinned at her, quirking his brows.

Bree rolled her eyes, but rubbed his hand at the same time. "Seriously. You're crazy."

"Yep. Fully admit it."

His phone buzzed just then, and he heaved a sigh, shaking his head. "Wanna check that?"

"I don't know, do I?" she shot back. "Who would it be?"

"Northbrook guys, probably. They've been texting a lot lately."

Bree released his hand to pick up the phone. "Oh yeah? Why's that? Code, please."

"Four-four-zero-five," he recited. "And because we reconnected, and the whole thing to save the club."

"Oh yeah." She made a sympathetic face at him. "Any progress?"

"Not yet. I'm thinking of asking Mr. White for more information or something, just to see how bad it is."

Bree nodded at once. "Do that. I can take a look; maybe I can help. Math runs in the family, you know."

Clint smiled fondly. "Yes, I know. Why and how anyone would let math do that is beyond me, but it's fine."

She stuck her tongue out, then returned her attention to the phone. "They're debating why you haven't responded to any of the messages. Some guy named Diesel thinks you're practicing your slapshot, since it's so weak."

"What?" Clint muttered incoherently under his breath in irritation for a minute. "Tell them I don't have time or interest in joining in their inane conversations . . . " He trailed off as he realized she'd already been responding. "What are you doing?"

Bree flicked her eyes over to him, her mouth curving into the most tempting, impish smile he had ever seen. "Telling them you're on a date with me and to keep things civil so I don't take it personally."

Clint's jaw dropped, and it was all he could do to keep his eyes safely on the road. "Bree Stone, are you crazy? Do you have any idea what that is going to unleash?"

She turned in her seat to give his profile a very direct look. "Clint McCarthy, I've grown up with the text conversations of the Six Pack as a norm. Do you really think your hockey buddies are going to scare me off?"

There was something insanely attractive about the set tone in her voice, but it didn't do anything for the fear swirling around his head.

The phone in her lap buzzed at least four times, and she checked the screen, giggling to herself.

"No, no," Clint warned firmly. "No secret laughing. You tell me what they are saying."

Bree cleared her throat. "Jax says it's about time you got a woman in your life. Dice wants a selfie on the date to prove it. Rock asks if I'm cute, which is more than a little presumptuous and inappropriate, in my opinion. And Diesel just sent a bunch of applauding emojis."

"Oh boy . . . " Clint pulled the car into a parking spot at their destination and turned the car off, turning to look at Bree very frankly. "You're in for it now, sweetheart. They'll be hooked, and there's no going back."

Bree smiled back and lifted a shoulder in a shrug. "Whoops." The phone buzzed in her hand, and she glanced down, her mouth popping open at whatever she read.

Great. "Now what?"

"Freaking Zamboni," Bree stammered.

"Tell me he wasn't inappropriate," Clint moaned, rubbing his forehead.

"Not really," she replied slowly. "He just . . . Well, he sent a lot of flame emojis, and then said he wants all the details later." She looked up at him. "You aren't going to tell him, are you? I don't know the others, but him . . . I'm still mad about that hit."

Clint took the phone, laughing. "You're the one who told me to be bigger than the hit!"

"I stand by that," she flat out said. "You need to be bigger than it. I never said I had to be."

That was the most adorable, the most hilarious, and unquestionably the best thing he had ever heard in his entire life, and he let himself laugh good and hard over it. Then he wiped at his eyes and responded to the text while saying, "My gosh, that was great. You are seriously the greatest, Bree, and I love that you said that."

"Glad I could be amusing," she muttered moodily. "What are you saying?"

He looked up at her as he hit send. "That my date is my

business, they should mind theirs, and I'd rather spend time with you than waste time with them."

Bree stilled in her seat, her eyes fixed on him. "Oh." She averted her eyes to look out of the windshield, then gasped. "Oh! We're here?"

Clint opened his door, still laughing. "We are indeed. Know why?"

She didn't wait for him to come to her door, jumping out and slamming the door behind her. "We aren't . . ."

"We are," he insisted. He offered her his arm like an old-fashioned gentleman. "Time to get you on the ice, my dear."

Bree took his arm but looked up at the Hawks' arena with apprehension. "I'm not sure about this."

"I am," he told her as they walked in. "No pressure, just us, and all the time in the world. Do you think I would let you fall? Or get hurt in any way?"

"No." She hugged his arm to her as if to prove it. "I'm just . . . I'm not very good about potentially embarrassing things."

Clint stopped and turned to face her, taking her other hand in his. "Hey, there is nothing embarrassing about learning, okay? If you really don't want to do this, we'll leave right now and go do something else tonight. No pressure, I promise."

Bree searched his eyes, then looked at the doors to the arena. "No," she murmured, almost to herself. "No, let's do this. I want to learn." She looked back at him, smiling almost believably. "Teach me how to skate, Clint."

He gripped her hands tightly in lieu of kissing that sweet smile senseless. "You got it, Breezy." He winked at her, then continued into the building, taking her to the rink, where he'd stashed the skates he'd brought up earlier in the day.

"How'd you get the whole arena?" Bree demanded as he

laced her skates for her. "There's got to be community rinks available we could have gone to."

"That's true, there are," he responded, tying a double knot before looking up at her. "But I couldn't get those to allow a private lesson. I know people here now, so it was way easier."

Bree scoffed a laugh at that, shaking her head. "Unbelievable. That's so much work just to save my pride."

"Have you ever stopped to consider," he asked as he worked on his own laces, "that it could be my pride I'm saving? I could be the worst skating instructor ever, and what would that do for my professional reputation?"

"Well, we couldn't have that." She shook her head in all seriousness. "So early in your pro career, appearance is everything."

He nodded in agreement. "Glad you think so." His skates were done in a moment, and he helped Bree to her feet. "Careful. You can walk fairly normally on the rubber; the blades aren't as unstable."

She started walking with him, and exhaled a quick laugh. "Such a weird feeling! Almost like wearing heels."

Clint hissed a wince, holding her hand as he stepped onto the ice. "Please, Bree, for the love of Pete, don't compare my career with wearing women's shoes."

Bree threw her head back on a laugh, her throat dancing with it. "Oh my gosh, Clint! That isn't what I meant."

"You said it, not me." He turned to face her, holding his other hand out. "Although the guys would have a riot with that comparison."

"Feel free to share it." She looked at the ice, then exhaled roughly. "Here goes nothing." Placing her other hand in his, she stepped out onto the ice, almost slipping immediately. "Whoa!"

"I've got you. Don't worry, I've got you." He slowly skated backwards, steadying her wildly unbalanced beginning. "Relax. Don't look at the ice; look at me. It never works if you start off panicking."

Bree met his eyes, a mixture of fear and amusement in her hazel eyes. "And how would you know? Have you ever panicked on the ice?"

He nodded with a smile. "Sure. Five is a very terrifying age for all activities."

"Shut up." She laughed a terrified breath, her grip on his hands almost painful. "Okay, on the ice. Now what?"

"Relax your knees," Clint instructed gently. "Feet a little further apart, point your toes slightly out."

She struggled to manage that without picking up the skates from the ice, as she would have done on a flat surface, but she eventually got it. "Okay . . . "

"Good." He slowed his glide, using his left hand to grip and indicate her right hand. "With this foot, put a little pressure to propel yourself forward. You can turn it further out for more stability if you need."

Bree's tongue flicked out as she thought it out, twisting her foot almost too far out to the side. "Okay . . . "

"And push."

She nodded once. "And push."

She pushed off, shooting forward with more force than either of them expected, and slammed into his chest, sending them both moving and losing her balance.

Clint gripped her arms to keep her from falling as he fought for a grip on the ice himself. "Whoa, whoa . . . "

She gripped him tightly, her breathing laced with nervous whimpers.

"I've got you," he insisted, regaining control and stabilizing them both. "Hear me?"

Bree looked up, and it was only then that he realized that she was right there. Flush against him. Clenching his jacket. Her lips literally hovering beneath his.

His attention was drawn there, and his own lips buzzed as they felt the faint pant she released. It would be so easy... *so* easy to dip his head and kiss her, gently and thoroughly and for a very long time. Here on the ice, where he was at home, with her in his arms.

It would be perfect beyond his wildest imagination.

He dragged his eyes back to hers, only to find her attention on his mouth as well.

Heaven help him...

"I've got you," he breathed as he held her still.

"Yeah," Bree whispered, her eyes dark as they traveled up to his own. Another breathless release of air. "Yeah, you do."

Clint was going to die here on this ice. That was the long and short of it, and it was going to happen no matter what he did.

Death by Bree.

He cleared his throat, squeezed her arms gently, and slid his hands down to hers as he scooted back. "Let's try that again, shall we?"

Bree nodded and pushed herself forward much more confidently, squealing with delight when she did so.

"Attagirl!" Clint praised, releasing one of her hands, watching her skates. "Don't lift your skates so much; just let them glide. They'll fall back into a good push off. Don't force it."

She listened with perfection, bringing her skates parallel at the right times, pushing off with ease and holding his hand with less panic. "How do I go faster?" she asked with a tentative grin.

"That takes some practice," he told her, laughing. "But if you trust me..."

Her smile deepened. "Of course I do."

A lump formed in his throat, and he fought to rid himself of it. "Okay." He moved around behind her, putting his hands on her waist. "Hold on."

Her hands instantly went on top of his. "Got it."

Clint shook his head, exhaling silently to himself. So this was what it felt like to die a glorious death.

So be it.

Gently pushing against her, he pushed off the ice and propelled them both forward, murmuring instructions to her while he provided the force as they made their way around the rink. It wasn't smooth, and it wasn't graceful, but it was something special. They laughed, they joked, and when they inevitably fell, they got back up together and continued to skate around hand in hand.

Just because.

THIRTEEN

ENOUGH WAS ENOUGH.

She couldn't even focus on her schoolwork anymore, Clint was so distracting. Deadlines and internship plans hung over her head, and all she wanted to do was be with Clint. Go to his games, watch his practices, hang out at his place and watch old footage of him, wander around campus aimlessly while she rambled about nothing . . .

Sitting in class was pure torture these days, and Bree hated that.

Hated it.

School was something she had always enjoyed, even if the subject material of her classes hadn't been particularly thrilling. She loved being a student and loved learning, and she'd inherited that from her dad, at least. She had never, in her entire life, been so distracted by a guy that school became almost insignificant.

She'd made a habit of silently judging the girls in her high school that had done just that.

Now here she was doodling in her notebook again rather than listening to Dr. Glass.

She didn't even know what the lecture was about today, but she was sure it would be on his final exam.

Did she care? No.

Should she care? Probably.

Would anyone agree with her?

Not in her house, anyway. Penny and Amy seemed to be living vicariously through her, and the fact that Clint had yet to kiss Bree or Bree to kiss him was literally driving them insane. Penny threatened to show up at their next date with a mob to chant "Kiss, kiss, kiss" until they complied, of all things, though Bree vowed she was going to sneak out for her next date just to keep her roommates in ignorance.

She didn't trust Penny not to have a tracking device on Bree somewhere to make it happen regardless.

Bree was a little frustrated about the situation herself, but it was more than that.

She was flat out, head over heels, all-the-heart-eyes in love with Clint McCarthy. She hadn't even kissed the man, and she already knew that. Felt that. Lived with that.

What exactly that meant was less certain.

She'd never been in love before, not really. Infatuation, sure, but her experience with guys was limited at best and pathetic at worst. How in the world did anyone know for sure how they felt or what it was or what to do about it?

The only person she would even consider confiding all this to was Trista, and there was absolutely no way she could tell the wife of a Six Pack member that she, a Six Pack Sib, was in love with another Six Pack Sib. Especially when she had nothing to back it up. The havoc it would wreak among the Six Pack alone made Bree queasy.

But a more stubborn voice inside of her demanded to know why *her* life had to be dictated by the Six Pack.

And that was a very good question.

She checked her phone as unobtrusively as possible, then gathered her things and slipped out of the classroom, breathing a sigh of relief when she reached the outside. Normally she would never leave class early, but it was the only time her advisor could meet to discuss her progress with the internship she needed to have next semester.

It would be a short meeting; Bree *had* no internship set for next semester.

There were only a few weeks left in the semester, and literally everyone else in her program had something set. She had interviewed for a few places, but nothing felt right; nothing would give her the experience and the education she wanted for her future.

What exactly she did want was up for debate.

Figuring that out was something she'd put off all semester.

She couldn't put it off any further.

Shaking her head, Bree zipped up her fleece against the chilly breeze as she crossed the square to her advisor's building. If all else failed, she could always see if her mother's nonprofit needed an intern.

Spending a semester in Baltimore sounded horrible, given that Clint would be in St. Louis, but maybe separation would make things sweeter?

Or maybe it would end things. If things were going to end anyway, she might as well have it end early.

The thought brought a stab of icy pain to her chest, and she shook her head as she entered the building and headed down the hall.

She didn't want things to end with Clint.

Maybe ever.

What did that tell her?

Her advisor's office was before her, and Bree knocked softly.

"Come in."

Pushing the door open, she smiled at the woman behind the desk. "Dr. Pershing, you wanted to meet?"

"Yes, Bree, come on in." She stood and gestured to a chair across from her. "Sorry to pull you from Dr. Glass's riveting class, but I'm concerned."

Bree sat, sliding her bag to the floor. "About?"

Dr. Pershing gave her a knowing look. "You have no plans for next semester. This is an internship program, Bree. You have to have some sort of position set up for a majority of the semester."

"I know," Bree sighed, not bothering to hide her reluctance.

"What's holding things up?"

Bree shrugged, then shook herself and sat up, forcing herself to be more confident than the shy little girl she was acting like. To take responsibility for herself. To be the adult she ought to be. "Honestly, I don't know what I want to do. I don't know which direction I want to go, and that makes finding an internship hard. I don't want to waste anybody's time doing something that won't help me or something that I don't like."

Dr. Pershing gave her a pitying look. "Nothing is going to be perfect, Bree. It's about the experience."

"But it is also about the network," Bree insisted. "I've read the stats. Most of the candidates wind up getting a job at the same company after their internship, if they've done a good job. I haven't found anything yet that I would want to continue to work at after the semester is done."

"I see." Dr. Pershing sat back, twisting her lips in thought. "Any thoughts at all? Even basic ones?"

Bree heaved a sigh, her fingers drumming on the arms of the chair. "I think I want to go nonprofit, but that doesn't exactly narrow things down."

"No, it doesn't. But I do have a decent list of nonprofit connections. If I send it to you, will you promise me you will look into these options? I don't want you to get into trouble next year because you don't have a position."

"I don't want that either." Bree nodded, drumming her fingers once more. "I'll look into them, absolutely."

Dr. Pershing smiled at her and returned her nod. "Good. I think if you give this your undivided attention, you'll figure something out."

Bree tried to return her smile, and she did her best, but something genuine wasn't possible. She shook her advisor's hand and left the office, fake smile fading.

Undivided attention, was it?

Unfortunately, her undivided attention was focused on Clint McCarthy at the present, and that was going to be particularly difficult to shift.

If not impossible.

Bree exhaled through buzzing lips, frowning to herself. Why did everything have to be so confusing? Why couldn't she compartmentalize and have internship time and Clint time? She could manage dividing herself between the two, couldn't she?

Her phone buzzed then, and she reached for it, answering without looking. "Hello?"

"Hello there," Clint's warm voice soothed her, with instant ripples of delight cascading through her. "Busy?"

"Just got out of a meeting, actually," she replied with a smile.

"Ah. Good meeting? Bad meeting?"

"Neither," Bree admitted with real honesty. "I don't have

an internship for next semester, and my advisor is concerned. I've got to figure something out, or I could be in trouble. Program-wise."

Clint made a hissing sound. "Yikes. Can I help?"

Bree hesitated, then sighed a laugh. "Normally, I would say no, but that actually sounds amazing. Meet me at my place?"

"On my way. See you soon."

She hung up and picked up her pace, her smile spreading without any effort. Maybe she could kill two birds with one stone. Clint could investigate options with her, and for those that were out of the St. Louis area, she could get a decent read on him for if their relationship, whatever it was, could withstand a long-distance stint.

It was insane how much she hoped it could.

The walk back to her apartment was quick, and the sight of Clint's blue truck made her smile. There was no reason whatsoever for him to have a truck, but he loved it, and it seemed to fit him.

He was sitting in his truck, apparently waiting for her, and when she was close enough, he got out, pushing his sunglasses back on his head and grinning at her with all his glorious attractiveness. "Hey, you."

"Hey yourself." Her voice almost broke seeing him, for no reason whatsoever, and she cleared her throat, swallowing hard.

Clint's expression softened. "Need a hug?"

"Always." She moved into his open arms without hesitation, sighing in delighted relief when his arms cradled her tight against his broad chest. No matter what was going on in her life, no matter how stressed she might be, everything was right when she was in Clint's arms.

Absolutely everything.

"You okay?" Clint asked softly as his hands ran up and down her back.

The motions were doing less to soothe her and more to distract her, and it was all she could do to keep from arching like a cat into him in encouragement. Nobody needed her to do that. There was no telling where it would lead.

But what an intriguing idea...

"Yep," she said with a quick snap to her voice, pulling back and grinning at him. "I just like hugging you."

He smiled back, and she doubted he was fooled, but he only gestured to the house. "I like hugging you too. Holding you, really. And lots of other things. Skating with you ... eating with you ... "

"Stop it." She laughed, fumbling for her keys and unlocking the door. "Don't go through everything we've been doing. It'll take ages."

"I've got time, and I wouldn't mind a good reason to stay with you longer."

Bree turned around as she entered the apartment, widening her eyes. "Clint! Don't intentionally make me blush."

His grin was slow and curled her toes easily. "Why not? You're beautiful when you blush."

Oh boy. This might not be such a productive session researching internships at all.

Distraction. Distraction, quick...

"Oh," she said slowly, forcing a teasing note into her shaking voice. "So I'm beautiful when I'm embarrassed? That's great, that's really great. Attractive when I've made a fool of myself."

"That isn't what I said!" Clint laughed and sat himself down on the couch, watching her with a smile as she set her bag down and removed her jacket. "Some people blush when they're pleased, you know."

Bree raised a brow. "Do they?" She went into her room to grab her laptop and took the unobserved moment to inhale and exhale gulping breaths of air. If she wasn't careful, Clint was going to set her on fire.

She'd blush with pleasure then, for sure, and everything would spiral from there.

Breathing under control, Bree grabbed the computer and headed back into the living room. Clint hadn't moved, and his attention on her was particularly fixed.

Gulp.

"Want something to drink?" she asked, her voice too high as she moved into the kitchen, laptop still clutched to her chest.

"I'm good, thanks."

Oh. Great.

She grabbed a bottle of water for herself from the fridge and turned back around to face him. Memories from the other night on the ice flooded back, and she could feel his hands on her waist, the gentle pressure propelling them both forward on the ice. The cold breeze from their motion combined with the heat of him behind her had made for a frenzied whirlwind of sensations within her, something addictive and delicious.

Something she would never forget.

Something filling her again now.

"Bree," Clint suddenly began, sitting forward on the couch and rubbing his hands together. "I need to tell you something."

She was doused in icy waters while she stood there, the shock of her heated memories popping in various parts of her with distress. "Yeah?"

His smile was gentle, his eyes unreadable. "It's been just

a few weeks since that basketball game, and we've been seeing a lot of each other since then." He broke off for a wry chuckle. "A lot, actually."

She could only nod, her grip on her laptop and water bottle clenching.

"I've loved every minute of it," he admitted with a rough, almost raw tinge to his voice that made her knees shake.

"Me too," she heard herself whisper, though she couldn't actually feel her lips moving.

Clint paused at that, then began rubbing his hands together again. "I'm ... I'm never going to forget when I first saw you again. Standing there in the basketball concourse, your hands full of food, toe to toe with my teammates without any hesitation or intimidation. That alone would have impressed me, but ... "

He trailed off, and Bree could almost feel herself leaning towards him, silently begging him to go on.

She didn't like the sound of "but" after how he'd begun.

Clint laughed very softly, looking down at his still-moving hands. "I stood there like an idiot in the concourse, staring at you for a lot longer than I should have before I said anything to or about you. I couldn't believe it was you, but I knew it *was* you, and somehow that made you even more beautiful than what my eyes were seeing." His eyes dragged over to hers, and the intensity in their depths stole her breath. "It took me way too long to figure out what to even say to you until I got the opening I needed. I don't even remember what I said to you that night because all I could think of was how beautiful you were and how much of an idiot I felt like."

The trembling in her knees increased and she set the bottle of water down on the counter, if for no other reason than to steady herself.

"And then you hugged me, and I was a goner." His throat

worked on a swallow, and he nodded. "Knew then that things would be different. Better, I hoped. I was still speechless, but I knew."

Bree wet her lips very carefully, thousands of words tumbling end over end in her mind. "Nobody's ever been speechless over me before."

He shook his head. "Doesn't matter. I was. Still am. And the more time I spend with you, the more speechless I get."

Bree was speechless too. Speechless, breathless, senseless . . .

"I'm in this, Bree," Clint told her. "In for the long haul."

It was astonishing that she hadn't actually crumpled to the floor or melted into a puddle, but her legs were absolutely not going to take much more of this. She turned just slightly to set her computer down, drummed her fingers on the top, then turned to face Clint again, exhaling shortly.

"I think you'd better kiss me, Clint McCarthy. I think you'd better kiss me right now."

His eyes widened, and he pushed up to his feet, his mouth curving. "I was thinking the same thing, but I didn't want to presume . . ."

Bree nodded on a shaky inhale. "Seriously. Now."

Clint's shoulders dropped on a massive exhale, and he started towards her. "Finally."

She barely had time to gasp before his lips were on hers, pressing her back against the counter, one hand cupping her face and tilting it perfectly towards him. She grabbed for his shirt with one hand while the other snaked up to latch onto his neck. Her lips parted instantly for him, begging him to take full advantage, to drive her completely out of her mind until she forgot her own name.

He seemed well on his way. There was no hesitation, no tentativeness, no resistance. His lips caressed and molded against hers, his free arm going around her waist and fitting her to him with far more perfection than she could ever have imagined. She pressed up on her tiptoes, bringing her other hand to join the first, pulling him closer, forcing the kiss deeper, curling her fingers against the skin of his neck as her pulse raced.

Clint groaned and gave in to her, gave her everything, growled when she curled her fingers into his hair. He pressed her harder against the counter, his mouth gnawing at her lower lip, the corner of her mouth, running a ragged line to her jaw and niggling down to her chin, where he gently grazed the skin with his teeth.

Bree exhaled in delight, dropping her head back, her fingers sliding further against his scalp. She needed more, needed his mouth on hers, needed *him*.

She tugged his hair, forcing his mouth back up to hers. He lifted her to the counter, and she folded her arms around his neck, sighing against the wonders of his mouth.

He chuckled breathlessly and gentled his kisses, his lips turning tender, wringing pleasure from her and delivering more of the same. After the depth of his previous kisses, these were maddening to the extreme, and every slow graze of his lips sent swirls of energy coiling into the arches of her feet.

With a final gasp, her lips parted from his, exhausted and exhilarated after such a frenzy, and Bree touched her brow to Clint's, shifting closer to him, her arms still tight around his neck.

Clint exhaled with a soft whooshing sound, brushing his nose along hers. "Wow."

Shivering, Bree nodded against him. "Yeah. Wow."

"That's been building up, huh?"

She giggled, tightening her hold briefly. "Sure has. I thought I was going to come out of my skin."

"Yeah, I got that . . . " He leaned in for a slow, gentle kiss. "But the feeling was mutual, so . . . "

Bree rested her forearms on his shoulders and pulled back just enough to get a good look at him, her fingers playing with his hair a little. "I don't know how we're supposed to get anything done anymore. Ever."

He grinned, squinting just a little at her. "Are you saying you want to kiss me again, Bree Stone?"

She raised a knowing brow. "I've wanted to kiss you for a very, very long time, and now that I know what I'm getting into, I'm pretty sure I'll be in a constant state of dying to kiss you at any given time."

Clint's mouth dropped open, his entire frame stilling in her hold.

Bree laughed softly and pulled him in for one more kiss. "Is that okay with you?"

He swallowed, his fingers playing with the material of her shirt. "I believe the answer you are looking for is, 'Yes, ma'am,' but I am finding that hard to say when your heels are digging into the back of my knees and making my legs shake."

"What?" Bree glanced down, then burst out laughing. "Oh my gosh, I had no idea. When did that happen?"

Clint shrugged. "Somewhere between the beginning and the end—it's a little hazy—but I like being locked in like this." He grinned playfully, then moved his hand to gently grip her chin, drawing her in for yet another kiss.

But just a quick one.

"Okay," he said slowly, drawing the word out. "Now that that's out of the way, shall we try to be productive?"

Bree made a face. "Do we have to?"

He gave her a searching look. "You're the one with an internship to find. You tell me."

They stared at each other for a moment, then Bree slumped where she sat. "Yes, we have to."

He patted her waist soothingly. "Okay then. If you'll kindly release me..."

She very slowly did so, and he gave her a warning look that made her laugh. He returned to the couch and patted the seat next to him.

Bree sighed and hopped down from the counter. "Heard from your Northbrook guys?"

"Actually, yeah. I asked Mr. White for that information you wanted, and he sent me way more than I bargained for." He shook his head, widening his eyes as she came over. "No idea what to make of the mess, and I don't know how to save the club if I can't understand the details, but..."

An idea crashed into Bree's mind as she slowly sat next to Clint on the couch, her eyes seeing nothing as the information surrounding such an idea unfolded.

"Bree?" Clint prodded, his voice sounding very far off. "Breezy? Hey, babe, you in there?"

She blinked and turned her attention to him, still processing.

His brow furrowed. "Where'd you go?"

Bree bit the side of her cheek, slowly releasing it as the whirling of her mind slowed. "Could you pull all that information up for me? Like now?"

"Sure, but why?"

She handed him her laptop and curled up next to him, excitement filling her in a completely different way. "I'm having a thought that might solve a whole lot of problems, or create a bunch of new ones. Hopefully both."

FOURTEEN

Bree was incredible.

Clint had known that for some time, but the last few days had driven that point home with several exclamation points. Ever since she'd had the idea about Northbrook, she'd been on fire, wrapped up in thoughts and paperwork, typing away furiously. She barely came up for air or food, but the energy that he saw in her eyes and expression was the true magic.

She was more alive than he had ever seen her, and he hadn't thought she could get any more vibrant in his eyes.

The actual details of what exactly her great idea was, she had yet to share. She was insistent that she would tell him as soon as she had something concrete, but he had a fair enough idea just by the questions she asked.

She was taking on Northbrook. She had been looking at financial records, community reports, alumni of the program that had gone on to the pros, anything and everything surrounding Northbrook in any way, shape, or form. In the last few days, Bree had spoken to his parents five times as often as Clint had, all with random questions about Northbrook.

He'd never seen anyone so fixated on a project in his

entire life, but that was entirely Bree. Single-minded focus and an insatiable drive to see things through.

Just yesterday he'd caught the tail end of a conversation between her and her dad that had cracked him up to no end.

"I'm going to email you some numbers, and I was wondering if you could check them for me. Run an analysis, maybe."

There was a pause, followed by an exasperated sigh.

"Yes, Daddy, I know I could do this myself, and maybe even do it faster. That isn't the issue. I don't have *time* to do this bit, so if you . . . Thank you. Love you. Call you later."

He'd asked her about it, but she'd brushed him off with an airy "You'll find out" and kissed him in a way that made him forget he wanted answers to anything at all.

It was amazing, but after that first kiss with Bree, all Clint wanted was more kisses with Bree.

Years of them.

Ages of them.

She was more than accommodating in that regard.

He smiled now as he stepped off of the team bus, just getting back from a trip to Florida to play Jacksonville, who had killed them. Normally he wasn't thrilled coming home after a loss, but Bree made everything about coming home easier.

She wouldn't still be up this late, but he'd take her out to breakfast in the morning and hold her hand the entire time. It was just a habit; he needed to be continually touching her when they were together.

He'd never been the touchy-feely kind of person until now.

Until Bree.

Grinning, he pulled out his phone to send her a goodnight text, fully aware of how cliché and cheesy it was and not particularly caring.

He had a message waiting for him, but not from Bree.

Grizz: Call me. Now.

Clint's smile turned the slightest bit hesitant. He knew exactly what this was about but wasn't entirely sure he wanted this conversation.

There wasn't any avoiding it, but with a text like this, it wasn't going to be pretty.

It's late, he texted back, hoping his brother would be asleep by now.

When his phone almost immediately rang, he groaned but pressed the answer button anyway. "Why aren't you sleeping?"

"Because that was a jerk move you pulled, sending that kind of a text and then getting on a stupid plane so I couldn't call and demand an explanation."

"Aww, you stayed up just to talk to me?" Clint clicked his tongue as though he were growing emotional. "That is so sweet, Grizz."

His brother grunted darkly. "Shut up. Now, will you kindly explain to me what in the world you meant by 'I'm falling for Bree Stone'? Since when are you spending time with Bree?"

Clint grinned to himself as he climbed into his truck, tossing his bag in the back. "Is Rachel there? Is she going to be firing questions at the phone with you?"

"I'll have you know my wife is fast asleep in bed, and I would very much like to join her, so please . . . "

"There is no way your wife would be sleeping if she knew you were going to drill me about Bree, so clearly you didn't tell her." He gasped dramatically. "Are you keeping secrets from your wife?"

"Clint, I am very tired, it is very late, and I will very much pound you into oblivion next time you're up here. Please."

Sensing his brother was actually quite concerned about the situation, Clint gave him a break. "Okay, what do you want to know?"

"What the hell is going on? That's what I'd like to know."

Clint sighed heavily and turned on his truck, waiting a second for the Bluetooth settings to connect. "Okay. Bree and I have been seeing each other since before you all came out for my first game. We ran into each other at the basketball game. We sent the Six Pack a selfie."

"I remember, yeah."

"And . . . I dunno, Grizz, it just happened. I was addicted to being with her, *to* her. It's just been getting worse and worse, more and more and more . . ." He exhaled, sputtering his lips as he pulled out of the arena parking lot. "I don't even recognize myself anymore."

"Well, that happens. Rach hit me like a ton of bricks."

"I really shouldn't be saying this to you first, you know," Clint said with a laugh, "but . . . I'm in love with her. I am in love with Bree Stone. I don't say that lightly either. This is the real thing. The big time. It's been really fast and really intense, but man . . . it's real."

There was no sound from the other end of the line.

"Great," Clint muttered to himself. "Did I lose you?"

"No," Grizz said slowly, not entirely sounding like himself. "No, I'm here."

Clint scowled. "Perfect. Now I wish I had lost you."

Again, Grizz gave him a grunt. "Not that lucky, baby bro."

"Don't call me that." Clint shook his head and exhaled slowly. "Fine. Go ahead, say your piece. Let me hear it."

"Give me a minute," Grizz growled, and Clint could actually envision his brother rubbing his eyes while sitting at the kitchen table.

Poor Grizz, having to put so many words together so late at night over an exasperating younger brother.

"It can't be Bree, Clint."

That wasn't much of a surprise.

"Why not?"

"Because... because she's Bree!"

"Uh-huh. And it's precisely *because* she's Bree that I feel this way."

"Clint, you can't."

"Why not?"

"Six Pack."

Clint smiled tightly. "I'm not *in* the Six Pack. I've been telling you that for years."

"Seriously, Clint. You can't. Breaks so many rules."

"Says the man who fell for and married Rachel Bennett."

He had Grizz there, and the brief moment of silence testified to that. "That's different," Grizz mumbled.

"Oh," Clint said slowly, nodding in understanding. "Because you're actually a member of the Six Pack and she's the sister of one of your adopted brothers in the Six Pack? Yep. So different. Yours is much worse. I feel so much better now."

"Come on, man."

"Grizz, listen." Clint bit down on his tongue for a minute, searching for the right words. "I don't know how else to explain it, but it's precisely because of our association through the Six Pack that Bree and I have been able to... Well, that I, at least, have been able to feel so much so fast. We already knew each other and respected each other, and... I can promise you right now that if I had met Bree Stone just out of the blue, no Six Pack to force us together, I would still be addicted to her, invested in her, and in love with her. That's it, the end."

Silence met his ears in response to that. He wasn't going

to address it this time, though. The call hadn't dropped, and Grizz had heard every word he said.

Processing was allowed.

"You're set on this, huh?"

Clint grinned to himself. "Yep. All in. In fact, the more we talk, the better about it I feel."

"I'm getting off, then."

"Ha ha. So?"

"So . . . ?"

"Grizz."

His brother laughed, and Clint took that as a good sign. "You're not asking for my permission, and frankly, you don't need it. I love Bree. She's one of my faves. You want her, go for it. Hurt her, and no one will find your body, but that's roughly what I was told too."

"Thanks very much. So you'll help me figure out what to tell Ryker?"

"Absolutely not; you're on your own."

"I hate you."

"Good night to you too. Give Bree a big hug from me."

"Will do."

The call *did* disconnect at that point, and Clint exhaled very slowly.

One hurdle down, only a dozen or so more to go.

"Text Bree," he said out loud to his Bluetooth. "I told Grizz about us. Went great. Missed you. Sleep well." He cleared his throat, wondering why in the world he had a lump. "Send text."

The Bluetooth dinged in indication the text had sent, and Clint nodded to himself. They'd talked about letting their families in on their relationship, and they had agreed that someone should probably know sooner rather than later, just given the ties they had. Bree was terrified about telling Ryker, and Clint couldn't blame her.

Ryker wasn't particularly terrifying, but he was very protective of his sister, as he should be, and there was no telling who would be good enough for Bree in his eyes.

Clint wasn't sure he was good enough for Bree in his own eyes, but he was just going to go with that.

His phone rang suddenly, and he glanced at the alert on his dashboard.

Bree.

He pressed the answer button quickly. "Hey, beautiful, what are you doing awake?"

"Waiting for you," Bree murmured in a low, sleepy voice.

His hands tightened on the steering wheel while he fought against the jolt her words had given him. "Babe, you can't say things like that. Not nice."

"Thinking about you being home *is* nice."

"Breezy..."

She laughed, the sound even lower than normal, and it slowly trickled heat up his spine. "Sorry. So. Grizz is in?"

"Define *in.*"

Bree clicked her tongue. "Yeah... In with reservations, then?"

"I guess. He says to give you a big hug."

"That's sweet. So it's you he has a problem with."

Clint laughed as he came to a stoplight. "Apparently. How was your night?"

"Fine. Got a lot of stuff done, and potentially have an internship lined up."

"Hey, that's great!" He tapped his thumbs against the steering wheel to an imagined beat. "Going to tell me what it is?"

He heard her rustling. "Nope. Not until it's official."

"Come on," he groaned, turning through the intersection. "You're killing me, sweetheart."

"Well, it's not an actual internship!" she protested. "I'm having to get all kinds of permission to bend the rules, and I'm still waiting to hear back from the people I'd be working with on if they even want to do this..."

"They will," Clint assured her, feeling more magnanimous than anything else. "Whoever they are, whatever it is, they will want you. You are amazing, capable, and brilliant, and they will be lucky to have you."

Bree hummed softly, the sound ricocheting within his chest. "You're sweet. I like you a lot."

Clint smiled a big, stupid grin at that, not remotely embarrassed by how much satisfaction that gave him. "Well, I happen to like you a lot too. What do you say to that?"

He heard her yawn, and it made him chuckle. "I say it's too bad it's two in the morning, because I would love to see you."

"I'd love that too, baby. But you need sleep. Even brilliance must rest from time to time."

"Yes, we must, we surely must."

"You're adorable."

"You're crazy."

"Crazy for you."

Bree sighed a dreamy sigh, and he wasn't entirely sure it was pretend, which made his smile harder to remove. "You sure you can't come over?"

"I'm sure, much as I would love to. I don't think Penny would like finding me there in the morning."

"Penny's out of town."

"Now you tell me," he moodily answered as he pulled into the driveway of his condo. "How about I make it up to you?"

"Sounds promising. How?"

"Breakfast in the morning?"

"Mm. How early?"

Clint laughed, turning off the truck and clambering out. "Not too early, I promise. I have a wake-up practice at nine."

"That's just mean."

"It's fine. It's a short workout. I could swing by and pick you up after."

"Sounds like a plan."

"Good." He entered his condo and flopped himself down on the couch, sighing heavily, feeling the fatigue of a late night of traveling at last.

"You okay, babe?"

He smiled at the endearment, as he usually did. "I love when you call me that."

"You're fine."

"Thank you."

"Oh my gosh . . ."

He laughed once and opened his mouth, only to find the words he wanted to say stuck there.

He couldn't say it now. Not like this. Not over the phone. Not in the middle of the night.

"Clint?"

"Yeah, I'm here. You going to tell me about your top secret project soon?"

"Yes, actually. Can you do me a huge favor tomorrow?"

"Name it."

"I need all of your Northbrook guys in on a conference call or FaceTime. Think that can happen?"

Clint sat up, pressing the phone more tightly against his ear. "I think so. I'll check the schedules, but there should be some window that works. You need Mr. White, too?"

Bree hesitated on the other end of the call. "He already knows."

"He what now?" Clint looked at the phone, then put it back to his ear. "You serious?"

"Just . . . I'll explain everything I can tomorrow, okay? Can you get the guys?"

"Of course. Absolutely I can. Bree . . ."

"Yeah?"

He wanted to tell her. He wanted to tell her so badly.

He swallowed the words. "You're amazing, you know that?"

"I'm stressed and insane, that's what I am."

"Don't correct me when I'm complimenting you."

"Sorry."

He heard her yawn again and sighed. "Okay, my beautiful girl, you get some sleep, and I'll pick you up for breakfast tomorrow."

"I like the sound of that."

"Breakfast?"

"Huh-uh. Being your girl."

Clint looked up at the ceiling, then closed his eyes in an almost benediction. "You are. If you want to be."

"I want to be."

"Okay."

"Good night, Clint."

"Night."

He ended the call and tossed the phone onto the nearby recliner, then flopped back down onto his couch.

Bree Stone for the kill.

Points for her.

This was a dangerous game they were playing, but he was loving it. He hadn't lied; she was his girl. But more than that, he belonged to her. Whatever she wanted, wherever she wanted him, however she wanted him, he was hers.

He had no idea what she had planned for him and the

Northbrook guys tomorrow, and the fact that she had already been in communication with Mr. White showed him just how serious she was about this. He'd suspected, obviously, but for something to actually happen . . . for action to be taken . . .

It was becoming real.

He could only hope that her plans, as involved as they were, would be more realistic and plausible than the latest idea they'd had, which had involved selling all of Jax's dad's classic cars without telling him and giving the money to Northbrook.

They hadn't been serious, obviously, but all serious ideas would never have worked.

Bree might be able to do it, though.

Bree was just smart enough, just determined enough, just capable enough.

And she was his.

Who'd have thought?

Forcing himself to sit up, he pushed off of the couch and swiped his phone from the chair as he headed into the bedroom.

He pulled up the group chat for The Pit and started a message.

Clint: My brilliant gf has an idea for Northbrook. You guys free for a conference call tomorrow?

If he didn't have five solid responses in the morning, there would be hell to pay.

FIFTEEN

WHY, OH WHY, oh why had she told Clint she needed him to gather the Northbrook guys?

She wasn't ready for this. Couldn't be. What if the whole thing fell apart?

Bree shook her head as she straightened the living room for the fourteenth time. She had received permission from her advisor to use Northbrook as her internship so long as she continued to work on the project she had proposed.

The official presentation to her committee regarding that proposal was next week, but she had to move now to get the ball rolling. In order for her idea to work, she needed a number of things to go right and to happen quickly.

She would be letting these six guys in on the project she'd been furiously working nonstop on for a week, and only because she needed their help to get it to work. Her roommates were already working on various aspects in their area of expertise, and if everything went according to plan, they would be working together on this project all next semester too.

And for a long time after.

What had she been thinking?

That was a stupid question; she knew exactly what she'd been thinking. She was saving Clint's hockey club.

But the larger project wasn't about the Northbrook Elite Hockey Club.

It was about all athletic clubs.

Everything she had heard about Northbrook had centered around the surrounding community. Outreach to kids in need, camps to learn the basics of hockey from athletes playing at elite levels, regularly taking part in community projects and providing positive outlets for kids that might otherwise have nothing. It had changed a number of lives, not to mention trained some of the best hockey players in the professional and Olympic worlds.

She had contact information for every single one of them, and Mr. White had assured her that every one of them would help her, if they were able.

That, he assured her, was the power of Northbrook.

Bree hadn't tried that yet; she wanted Clint and his friends signed on first, and then they could help her decide who to reach out to next.

Clint had texted her that morning before his practice and told her all of the guys were available that afternoon, which had sent her into total work mode. She'd gone over the numbers her father had analyzed for her again, reviewed every document Mr. White had sent to Clint plus the ones she'd asked for herself, and clicked through every page of notes she, Amy, and Penny had put together since they'd taken all of this on.

She felt ready.

In theory.

A business meeting she could have handled.

FACEOFF

A meeting with her boyfriend's former teammates about saving one business and starting another ... not quite.

Almost, but not quite.

Clint had assured her at breakfast that she would be great, though he had no concrete idea what she would be proposing. Clearly it was about his club—there was no hiding that—but as for the rest ...

Was it ridiculous and juvenile for her to want him to be impressed?

A faint buzzing met her ears, and she felt for her phone in her pockets, but it wasn't there. She looked around the living room, scanning the well-worn couch and cushions to no avail.

"Phone," she muttered to herself, turning on the spot, her eyes grazing over every nook and cranny. "Phone, phone, phone, phone ... " The scanning stopped on the TV stand, where her black phone case blended almost perfectly with the wood and TV itself. "What in the world is it doing there?"

She hurried over to it and answered quickly. "Hello?"

"Hi, Bree," Trista's warm voice answered, not sounding quite as chipper as it normally did.

Bree exhaled, her shoulders sagging, and she moved over to the couch and dropped herself onto it. "Hi."

"So that was an interesting text," Trista said slowly. "Normally you're not that cryptic."

"Well, I didn't want some production assistant to know my business," Bree retorted with a smile. "So ... are you alone?"

Trista laughed softly. "Yes, sweetie, I am alone. I'm in my hotel room. We had a night shoot, so I'm free."

"Good."

Silence roamed the line between them, and Bree leaned her head back on the couch.

"Uh, sweetie . . . this thing only works if you actually talk."

Bree chuckled, then sighed. "I'm in love with Clint McCarthy."

Again, there was silence, but this time, it made Bree smile.

"Wow," Trista finally said. "Wow. I mean . . . that's so great, Bree!"

Bree sat up. "It is?"

"Yeah! I don't know Clint well, but I like him! And you know Grizz was raised right, so Clint will be too. How long have you two been a thing?"

A wince flashed across Bree's face, and she screwed up her eyes as she said, "Three weeks. Give or take."

There was a beat, and then a very slow "Okay . . ."

"I know. Trust me, I know." Bree covered her eyes on a rough exhale. "It's so fast. It's *so* fast, Trista. But it's also intense. And I'm so head over heels over whatever. He's . . . he's everything. I . . . I love him. I love him so freaking much, and it scares me to death."

"Oh, Bree . . . Honey, why does it scare you?"

Bree swallowed a sudden wash of tears. "Because I want in. All in. I know it's fast and intense, but this is it for me, I know it. At least, I think I know it. I don't know . . . " She groaned and sank further into the couch. "I sound so pathetic."

Trista made a sympathetic sound. "No, sweetie, you're not pathetic. This is what it's like, unfortunately. So let me ask you this: What is it that makes you want to be all in?"

"It's so easy with him," Bree told her, dropping her hand from her face. "He knows what it's like to be a Six Pack Sib. He gets me. He's not pushy, he's actually interested in me . . . he makes me laugh . . . he just wants to be with me. Nobody has ever wanted that."

"That's how it should be, Bree."

"But . . . " Bree wet her lips, shaking her head. "Do I love him just because he's the first guy who's been really into me?"

"Go with your gut. What do you think?"

Bree closed her eyes, thinking back to every moment she could recall over the past few weeks. Everything Clint had done for her, every tension-packed moment, every kiss, lingering a moment longer on that magical first . . .

"Even if I'd had a dozen boyfriends before Clint, I would still know that he's different."

"There you go, then."

"But I'm still . . . I don't know, I'm still scared."

"Are you scared of the novelty or scared of the intensity?"

"Yes . . . " Bree admitted with a nervous laugh. "Both."

"How scared?" Trista asked with some concern. "Do you want out?"

Instantly Bree shook her head. "No! No, that's just it; I want *in*."

She wanted it so much she could barely get the words out, could barely breathe.

How could she possibly convey that to her sister-in-law?

"How in?" Trista's voice was full of curiosity now, the concern clearly taking a back seat.

Bree grinned at a sudden mental image. "I'd walk down the aisle now if he asked me."

There was a surprised cough from Trista. "Oh, Bree . . . wow."

"Don't tell Ryker!"

"Of course not, I'm not an idiot."

They both laughed for a moment more. "Honey, I think you know what your heart wants, and I think you're just scared to get that out in the universe."

"So what do you suggest?"

"Tell him you love him. And kiss him senseless. The order of those two things doesn't really matter; they go hand in hand."

Bree's face flamed, but she giggled knowingly all the same. "I'll see what I can do."

"Attagirl! I'm seriously so happy, Bree. This sounds promising. Keep me in the loop, okay?"

"Always. I love you, Trista."

"Love you too, hon. Bye."

Bree smiled almost dreamily as she hung up, the idea of kissing Clint senseless always a pleasant one. Telling him how she felt about him was terrifying in the extreme, but maybe, if she kissed him senseless enough, she might find some courage in there.

Maybe.

A knock at the door had her springing up from the couch with a combination of a gasp and a shriek. Her eyes darted to the clock, and her stomach settled only a little.

It was time.

She moved to the door and opened it wide.

Clint stood there, gorgeous and rugged with his scruff, and his crooked smile made her heart flip-flop.

There was nothing for a sentient female to do but sigh at a man looking at her like that. "Hey."

He stepped closer and took her gently by the waist, pulling her close. "Hey," he murmured just before his lips descended on hers, a soft, slow, stomach-igniting kiss.

He pulled back just as she started to lean in, then chuckled at her pout. "That is not nice," she scolded.

Clint winked, his thumb dipping at her lower lip before dragging to her chin. "Maybe not, but I couldn't resist. You can get back at me later."

Bree scowled and smacked his back as he passed her for

the couch, shrugging out of his leather jacket. "I will, too, as soon as I figure out where and how to strike."

He raised a brow as he sat. "I'll be on the lookout, then."

"Won't help. I'm way sneakier than you know."

His slow grin prompted one of her own. "Now, that sounds promising."

Bree only gave a suggestive quirk of her brows. "Doesn't it, though?"

Their rather tantalizing banter was interrupted by the unmistakable sound of a FaceTime call coming in.

Right. Business.

Clint pulled out a tablet and propped it up on the table, pressing the answer button. On cue, five squares appeared, only two of which were currently filled with faces. The rest were pastel colors with a single letter in the center.

"What in the world?" Bree muttered, coming over to investigate.

"Group call," Clint explained with a laugh. "So much easier than trying to use multiple devices. And this way, everyone can actually see you, which is all the better for them."

Bree frowned and lightly whacked his arm.

"YES!" one of the faces on the tablet cheered. "Hit him again!"

"Hey!" Clint protested.

The guy shrugged, his head tilting in just the right way to reveal a tidy man bun, despite the short hair at the sides of his head. "Sorry, I was caught up in the moment." He grinned and waved at Bree. "Hi there. Zane Winchester."

Bree gave him a tight smile. "Bree Stone. And . . . I was at the Hounds-Hawks game."

"Yeesh." He flattened his mouth out in a comical manner, his neck straining with it, his dark scruff even darker with the shadows. "My bad. Um ... Normally, I am much better behaved than that."

"No, you're not," the other square laughed. "Hi, Bree. I'm Jax."

Bree waved, her smile easier this time. "Hey. Nice beard."

Jax laughed and stroked it proudly. "I know, right?"

"Question," Zane asked, raising a finger. "Do you condition that thing?"

One of the other squares dinged, and another face appeared, this one more tanned, his eyes and hair darker by far than the others. "Party's here!" he exclaimed. Then, seeing Bree, he smiled. "Oh ... Hi there."

Clint rolled his eyes with a groan. "Bree, that's Rocco. Ignore him."

"Yep, ignore him," Zane agreed.

"And him," Clint added.

The other two squares winked on then, and Bree exhaled slowly. "That's everybody, right?"

"Yep. So Jax, Zane, Rocco, Declan, and Trane," he recited, pointing to each in turn. "Guys, this is Bree."

"Hi, Bree," they all said in unison.

She snorted softly. "Suddenly this meeting took a very different turn ... "

"I like her," Trane pointed out amid the easy laughter from the rest.

"Good for you," Clint shot back.

Bree shook her head in amusement and resignation. Boys.

"Okay, I don't want to take up too much of your time," she said, her voice turning formal, "so I'm just going to get right down to it. Clint told me about what's going on with Northbrook, and having been raised in a sports-loving family myself, I wanted to help."

"Wait, wait, wait ... " Zane interrupted, his eyes widening. "You're not Ryker Stone's sister, are you?"

Bree sighed and nodded. "Yep."

"Dude!" at least three of the guys said at the same time, now looking at Clint with new appreciation.

"The Ryker Stone fan club doesn't meet until after this," Clint told them all firmly, his mouth curving in a smile. "Can it."

There were several snickers and scowls at that.

"Anyway," Bree went on, clearing her throat, "I should preface: I'm getting a master's in public administration, and my undergrad was business with a finance minor."

Someone whistled low in appreciation, and she took a moment to nod her thanks, which made them smile.

"Basically, I've been going over numbers and data for a week nonstop." She smiled over at Clint briefly. "My boyfriend is getting a little annoyed about it."

He coughed in mock dismay but put his arm around her anyway. "Never in a million years, babe."

"Cute," Rocco said blandly. "Moving on."

Bree returned her attention to them, turning serious. "I've been emailing back and forth with Mr. White, and I may have something that will work. Still working out several kinks, and there will probably be more popping up as we go. But ... I want to start a nonprofit."

She was met with five blank stares. Six, if one counted Clint.

"Northbrook is already a business," Jax pointed out, his frown visible even through his beard. "Its own entity. It doesn't need ... "

"I know," Bree overrode, an apology in her eyes. "I'm not trying to take over Northbrook or anything; I just think it needs help. And then it needs sustaining. At the moment, though, it's out of money and out of support. That's the hurdle we're facing at the present, and I've been working it out with my roommates, who are in public relations, advertising, organizational leadership, and business management."

Declan sputtered softly. "Dang..."

Bree smiled. "We've decided that there is a simple multistep process we can implement to keep Northbrook from folding and then restore it to what it was. The first focus is going to be temporary funding."

"Makes sense," Jax broke in with a nod. "But that's where the hang-up is."

"Not if we get creative," Bree countered firmly. "Between the seven of us, I think we can pull enough family, friends, and alumni alone to give us a big step."

"And do what?" Zane asked. "Ask for donations?"

"Kind of." Bree smiled, her excitement for the idea growing. She just needed them to catch on. "A fundraising event. A gala, if you will. Something big in Chicago, full fancy dress, red carpet, big names, the works. A night honoring Northbrook as it was and as it could be."

Clint released a thoughtful grunt of consideration. "I like it. Is one event going to be enough, though?"

"I doubt it," Trane said, looking less enthused. "They're deep in the hole financially."

"Correct," Bree agreed. "Which is where you guys come in."

"Jax is the moneybags," Zane pointed out at once.

It seemed that every other guy rolled his eyes at that, making Bree laugh. "That's not quite what I meant."

"Thank you," Jax retorted, looking a little redder at the moment.

"Then what?" Rocco asked her, leaning forward on the table he sat at.

Bree gave them all a quick grin. "Your influence."

"I'm listening," Zane replied with a smile.

"You all have connections in the hockey community," she explained. "And hockey fans. This is all about saving a hockey program. People need to see their own peewee years in Northbrook. They need to feel that this club could be their club. We need public support."

She looked at each of them directly now. "This is your story. Time to share it. Anybody have objections to being in a video we plan to make viral?"

"Nope," most of them said.

Trane, however, looked hesitant. "Maybe," he said slowly. "My story is a little different."

"Fair enough," Bree replied, trying for an understanding smile. "Can you work up something for me about what you're comfortable talking about or being asked?"

"Absolutely." He nodded firmly and returned her smile.

"Focus two," she went on, "getting back to community basics. We have to remind them what Northbrook has done and can do. Again, we need attention. Fundraising buys us time; we need a regular cash flow."

"What about doing some camps at the facility?" Jax suggested. "I'm in the area; it would be easy enough to make happen."

Bree pulled her notebook from the table and jotted it down. "Perfect! Would you mind looking into that and taking it on?"

"No problem."

"You're going to need a functioning board at Northbrook," Clint reminded her. "Mr. White is the only one right now."

She looked at him with a shy smile. "I know. I kind of already put your dad in charge of recruiting for that."

"What?" He burst out laughing while the others cheered. Bree eyed their reactions, her smile growing.

"Papa McCarthy is on it!" Declan exclaimed, pumping a well-muscled arm into the air.

Bree bit her lip, returning her attention to Clint. "And your mom is canvassing local businesses."

Now Clint fell back against the couch, his hands going over his face as he laughed.

"This is a beautiful thing," Rocco said with a sigh. "Any time you want to do anything behind Clint's back, I'm in."

"Thank you," Bree told him dryly. She looked down at her notes. "Oh, and I was wondering . . ."

Clint dropped his hands. "Uh-huh . . ."

She glanced over at him. "What if we pulled *our* strings?"

He slowly sat up, a faint furrow between his brows. "The Six Pack?"

"Uh-huh. They should all be able to come to the gala, in theory. They pull a lot of weight in the media, and if Cole can get a certain someone with certain credentials to help us with certain media outlets . . ."

Clint was already nodding, his smile bright. "She totally would. And if you can get a certain mega star to attend . . ."

"She absolutely would."

"Talking in code is only fun if everyone knows it," Zane announced with childlike whining.

"Daddy!"

All conversations stopped, and all pairs of eyes were fixed on the screens before them.

Except for one.

"Yeah, baby?" Zane called over his shoulder.

"I can't find Princess Dolly, and I've looked *everywhere*." A little girl with bouncing brown pigtails and a pink-on-pink ensemble ambled into their view of Zane, startling every single one of them.

Zane smiled and waved her over. "We'll go on a hunt for her when Daddy is finished with his call, okay? Want to say hi?"

The little girl climbed up onto Zane's lap, and he adjusted his camera to center them both.

"Hi there," Bree said after getting over the shock. "What's your name?"

"Hope," came the confident reply. "Daddy, are these your friends?"

Zane nodded, his demeanor completely softened now that she was there. "Yep. Daddy learned how to play hockey with these guys."

"Even the girl?"

That broke the ice perfectly, and they laughed. "No, honey, that's Bree. She's a new friend."

Bree felt her wariness about Zane melting away by the moment, and she grinned at the precocious little girl. "Hey, Hope, how old are you?"

Hope held up a hand with all five fingers extended.

"Five?" Bree confirmed. "That's the perfect age. Hope, can I ask you a favor?"

Hope's eyes brightened, and she nodded eagerly.

"Will you come to a big, fancy party I'm having with your dad and all of these guys? I could use another girl around, you know?"

The little girl gasped and turned to her dad. "Can I, Daddy? Please?"

Zane looked at Bree uncertainly. "You sure? Not quite a gala with . . . "

"Completely sure," Bree replied. "The more the merrier. Besides, Northbrook's always been about family, right?"

Five grins met hers on the screen. "Right."

SIXTEEN

"Thanks, Tyson. I owe you."

Clint smiled as he ended the call, putting his phone down on the armrest.

"That sounded promising."

He looked over at Bree, sitting against the opposite armrest of his couch, her bare feet tucked against his thigh, her attention completely devoted to her laptop. He smiled to himself as her fingers flew across the keys at an incredible pace, a wrinkle creasing her brow. "Tyson says he'll take care of it. I guess the guys from his year are still in good contact, and he's the unofficial leader. He's got a huge alumni list, guys that I had completely forgotten about."

"Perfect," Bree answered without looking up. "Does he think they'll come?"

"He said he'll make them."

Bree's hazel eyes flicked up to his with a smile. "Really?"

Clint nodded, then reached for Bree's feet and pulled them into his lap, tugging a leg to bring her closer.

"I can't come much further and be upright," she laughed, one foot pushing against him playfully.

"So don't be upright."

That earned him a dark look that made him laugh.

"Fine, fine, I'll come to you." He made a show of scooting closer, though it was only a matter of inches. He ran his hand over her ankles soothingly, then picked up one foot and began to rub, kneading the sole with his thumbs.

"Mmm," Bree moaned, biting her lip. "My gosh, that feels good. But you had a game tonight; you don't need to do this."

"Sure I do."

She hissed as he hit a particularly tender spot, prompting him to work at it a bit more. "But aren't you tired and sore?"

Clint shrugged. "A little of both, but I'm comfortable sitting here, and you're hard at work. I might as well help you relax and feel better. You've been under a lot of stress lately."

"Has it been that obvious?" she asked softly, a smile still on her lips, concern in her voice.

"No," he assured her, his fingers moving up to work through her toes. "I just noticed. And after that meeting today, I realized just how much you were getting done."

Bree made a quiet, noncommittal noise. "I wasn't doing it by myself. Penny and Amy have been working just as hard, and Mr. White has been on top of it, not to mention . . ."

"Stop," Clint told her gently. "Give yourself some credit, hon. This is a huge undertaking, and you are nailing it." He flashed a quick grin. "Besides, I wouldn't want to rub anyone else's feet but yours."

"I'd have to hurt you if you did." She returned his smile, then sighed. "I don't know about nailing it, honestly. Like I said in the meeting, I have no guarantee that any of this will work."

"Northbrook?"

Her eyes lifted to his. "Any of it. The fundraiser should work, sure, but this was never a question about raising money right away. This is a long game we have to play, and I feel like we're scrambling for the first bit."

Clint continued to rub her feet tenderly, pressing harder when he found a good spot, watching her reactions to guide his attentions. She was far more stressed than she was letting on, but her feet were certainly revealing a certain level of tension she never would have vocalized.

"The first part of the game is always a mad rush," he reminded her. "Faceoff is intense, first plays set the tone, and we want to get everything done right away."

Bree nodded, folding her arms against herself. "Yeah. I just . . . What if I can't pull this off?"

"Is that what's worrying you?"

Again, she nodded, and this time he saw her throat work on a swallow.

He held out a hand and beckoned her. "Come here."

She set her laptop aside and crawled over to him, resting on her knees beside him on the couch.

He took her face in his hands, forcing her eyes to meet his. His thumb stroked her cheek without thinking, and she leaned into his touch.

"No matter what happens," he told her gently, "you are extraordinary, and I am so proud of you. Beyond proud. I want to throw you a freaking parade just for being you."

Bree scoffed softly and rolled her eyes, but she pressed one of her hands to his while it rested on her face.

Clint smiled. "Do you want to know what The Pit had to say after your meeting today, before we all went off to our games? They wanted to know how I managed to find you, asked if you were real, and begged me to tell you that they will do absolutely anything you ask them to do. In case that wasn't already clear from how they were jumping to volunteer for things in your focus areas."

Her eyes lit up, searching his with an eagerness that warmed his heart. "Really?"

"Really," he confirmed with a sage nod. "I promise you, no matter what happens, you are still amazing, incredible, and brilliant. If Northbrook goes under after all of this, we can say we went down fighting. And it won't change anything for me, you know. About you."

Bree's smile turned almost dreamy before she leaned forward and kissed him, her lips capturing his over and over again in a slow, sensual dance. She hummed a small laugh and touched her brow to his, then surprised him with a quick kiss to his brow before returning to her spot on the couch and grabbing her laptop once more. Then she propped her feet back in his lap again.

"Really?" he asked with a laugh, taking up the other foot to begin working on it.

Bree's slender shoulders lifted in a shrug, her mouth curving to one side. "You can't leave me unbalanced."

"Heaven forbid."

He leaned his head back against the couch as he continued to rub her feet, thinking back to the meeting they'd had earlier in the day.

Bree had laid everything out for the guys, a game plan for getting Northbrook back on its feet, ideas for advertising, outreach projects she was looking into, and even some thoughts on generating revenue in a way that could conceivably make a difference there. She had listened to their thoughts and ideas, written every single one down, and built upon them. Every concern they had brought up, she had an answer for and had already considered.

He hadn't just been trying to bolster her a moment ago; she really was that impressive. He had seen Bree in her element, alive with ideas and plans and goals. She had taken charge without ever announcing she was doing so, and she had put things in order in a way that would have taken the six of them ages to do.

He couldn't remember what each of her focuses were, but the tiered approach she had presented had been genius. More than that, it had been professional, and it felt right.

Everything felt right.

Clint looked over at the remarkable woman beside him, now completely engrossed in her work once more, that adorable furrow back in place.

"What are you working on now?"

"Gala invites," she answered while gnawing on her lip. "And going through old photos of the facilities and clubs to find what would work best."

"At the same time?" he laughed in a low tone.

She smiled without looking up. "Multitasking, babe. It's my superpower. Plus your sister-in-law offered to actually plan the gala, so I'm prepping files for her. Fantastic that she's got a wedding planner in her family, you know?"

Clint nodded sagely, though he wasn't entirely sure which of his sisters-in-law she was talking about. Definitely not Rachel, it was safe to say, but he couldn't remember the details of the extended families of the other two. He loved them, of course, and they were fantastic partners for his brothers. He just didn't know which of the two would actually want to plan this thing in such a short amount of time.

He'd find out when one of his brothers called to get after him for saddling his wife with so much work.

"Anything I can do to help?" he offered as he continued to rub through her feet, loving the experience of touching her like this, keeping connected with her even while her mind was elsewhere.

"You're helping a lot right now. Besides, you played an amazing game today. Take a breather."

He smiled at her, though she wasn't looking. "It's great to have you at the games even with everything you're working on."

That made her smile, her attention still on her work. "I'm not missing a single home game. My man is a star, and I have no problem letting the world know it."

Her man.

No position, title, or label had ever sounded so perfect to his ears. That was what he wanted above all else, above his career, saving Northbrook, or any other ambition he might have for himself.

He wanted Bree. He wanted to be hers.

Being here with her, just like this, felt more right than any feeling he had ever known in his entire life. Sitting together after a long day, not even doing anything, but just being . . .

He could be with her just like this for the rest of his life.

He *wanted* to be.

This comfortable. This simple.

This beautiful.

And suddenly he couldn't wait one moment more.

"Bree?"

Her sprints of typing continued. "Hmm?"

Clint swallowed hard, his eyes on her. "I love you."

"'Kay."

He raised a brow, fighting a smile at the absent response, and dug his thumb into the sole of one foot hard.

The typing stopped, and Bree's eyes froze on the screen. Her toes flexed against his hand, and then her chin jerked up, her eyes wide. "Wait, what?"

He smiled fully at her, his hands resting now on her feet, holding them in place. "I love you," he said again.

Bree stared at him, her chest moving unsteadily with every breath beneath her tank top, the unbuttoned sides of the overlaying flannel shirt almost waving with the motion. Keeping her eyes on him, she slid her laptop back over on his coffee table, gently tugged her feet out of his hold, then pushed up on her knees.

He turned towards her, anticipation pumping through his veins.

Bree laced her fingers at the back of his head, then pulled him to her for a hard, deep, completely thorough kiss that unmanned him from head to toe. "I love you too," she whispered, when she let him up for air or thought. "So much. So much it scares me."

His hands, hovering at her waist in his state of suspended euphoria, now wrapped around her and pulled her body closer. "Don't be scared," he murmured, still fighting for breath. "I'm in this with you. We're together every step of the way. I'm all in for you, Bree."

Her grip on his head tightened, and she gave him another fierce kiss, her fear and exhilaration tangible in her lips and in the taste of her. "I'm all in too. Wherever this goes, you've got me, okay?" She folded her arms around his neck and buried her face into his shoulder. "You've got me."

Clint cradled her against him, turning her so she sat across his lap, content just to hold her this tightly, this possessively, for the rest of his life. "I've got you, Bree," he whispered into her hair. "I've got you."

She nodded against him and sighed, leaning into him more fully.

They held onto each other for what could have been hours, Clint wasn't about to keep track of the time. Bree was so relaxed against him, yet her arms never wavered in their hold on him. He didn't mind; this was undoubtedly the best he had ever felt in his entire life, and he doubted anything in the world would ever top it.

It couldn't.

"Not that I'm complaining," Clint murmured, pressing his lips to Bree's ear, "because this is the best part of my day..."

She snickered against him, then pulled back, lacing her hands behind his neck and leaning back against his arms. "I should hope so..."

"But are you going to work any more tonight?" he went on, ignoring her comment completely.

Bree shook her head firmly. "Nope. I'm done for."

Clint chuckled and leaned in for a soft kiss that made her hum. "Poor you."

"Do you want me to do more work?" she asked with a raise of a brow. "I can, if you'd rather I move..."

"Don't you dare," he warned as he clamped his hands more firmly around her, keeping her in place. "I just don't want you to be stressed out if you don't get stuff done."

Bree shrugged in his hold, her fingers moving up to play in the hair at the back of his head. "Most of the work is done tonight. I was just working ahead. Penny's doing all the social media and promo stuff, and the gala details aren't really on my plate anymore..."

"Good," he grunted, shifting her closer. "I don't want you to take too much on, even if you are Superwoman."

"Trust me, I'm not." She smiled at him, her fingers still sending sparks down his spine. "Got any ideas for making this all take off?"

He pretended to think about that. "Hmm... I could start a social media campaign with stupid athlete videos. Grizz might do it with me, if I blackmail him."

Her hand smacked lightly against the back of his head,

which made him laugh. "Oh, like that would do any good," she drawled, her voice dripping with sarcasm. She shook her head, sighing at him. "You're such a dork."

"Guilty." He gave her a cheeky grin, then ran a gentle hand over her hair. "Can I ask you something?"

"You keep playing with my hair and you can ask me anything," she practically purred.

Clint laughed and moved his hand back through her hair. "You said in the meeting you wanted to start a nonprofit, but we never got back around to that. What are you thinking, babe?"

Bree sobered and slid one of her hands down to his chest, fiddling with the buttons and collar of his Henley. "I want to do what we're doing with Northbrook."

"Saving hockey clubs in trouble?"

She dipped her chin in a nod. "Not just hockey, though. All clubs. Any activity organization in trouble. I want to provide temporary funding, sponsorship, business analysis, management strategies, restructuring . . . whatever is needed, really. I want to be the group that keeps sports programs from dying out. I want to restore these programs to their communities. Breathe new life into them."

Clint stared at the incredible woman in his arms, marveling at the idea and at her dedication to such a cause. He would never have thought of any such thing, but she had taken a situation that had been brought to his attention and not only come up with a plan for it but found a passion in it to fuel her future. She was going to make a world of difference in the lives of so many, and he had no doubts at all that she would not only be successful but thrive.

"What do you think?" Bree murmured, her eyes and fingers still on his collar.

He shook his head in disbelief and placed a finger under

her chin, tilting her face up to his. "I think you are brilliant," he told her, stroking the tender skin. "I think it's a fantastic idea, and I fully support everything about it. I think you are going to change the world, and I think I am the luckiest guy in the world to be so in love with you."

Bree's lips curved into a small smile, relief setting into every feature. "Yeah, you're pretty lucky."

That made him laugh out loud, which made Bree giggle in his arms. "Thank you very much."

"You're lucky," she said again, tugging at his collar, her smile turning into something playful and seductive that made his breath catch, her eyes darker than he could ever remember them being, "because I happen to be ridiculously in love with you. And I have never said that to anyone before. Just you."

For some reason, that did Clint in more than anything he had heard yet, and he pulled Bree in, his mouth finding hers with a familiarity and ease that warmed him. Her lips were soft and pliable but eager and wanting. She curved into him, her soft sighs and sounds snapping every ounce of sanity he possessed, pulling him further and further into the incomparable, addictive mystery of all that she was.

Bree suddenly pulled back and sat up with a heavy, satisfied sigh. "Well, it's getting late. I better get home so you can get a good night's sleep before practice tomorrow."

Still burning in various scattered parts of him, Clint stared at her in shock while she collected her things and put on her shoes. "What?"

She turned to look at him, expression superior and teasing. "I told you I would get you back, babe. Don't start a fire you aren't going to put out." She quirked her brows, blew him a kiss, then strode to the door.

"Let me walk you out," he sighed, pushing himself up.

She turned on the spot, backing towards the door. "I

think you've had enough kisses for one night, Fido. You stay right there." She gave him a warning look and left without another look or word for him.

He loved that woman, and it was a good thing he did.

That was a dirty trick.

Funny, deserved, but dirty.

He exhaled slowly, shaking his head, and leaned back on the couch, closing his eyes and going through the events of the day again. Amazing how his game had been the minor footnote in the day but had been one of his better games yet. He didn't mind one bit, particularly with what Bree had planned for Northbrook.

His eyes snapped open as a particular thought lodged itself into his mind, and the moment it solidified, he sat up and grabbed his phone, scrolling through his contacts and hitting the call button in a matter of seconds.

"Penny? It's Clint. Bree's on her way there, so we only have a minute. Tell me what you think about starting a social media campaign for all of this."

He smiled at her response. "Well, I'm glad you asked. Here's what I was thinking . . . "

SEVENTEEN

WEEKS OF PLANNING, hours of research, days of running around, and it all led up to this.

This night.

This event.

No pressure.

Bree shivered despite already being inside the Chicago hotel where the gala was being held, and the room being a warm enough temperature for a bitter-cold day after Thanksgiving. It was just the anticipation of the event and the fear that none of this would work.

After all of the work that she had put in, and her friends had put in, what if they fell short of their goals?

"Don't do that."

Bree turned to look at Penny, coming towards her in an elegant slate-blue gown that turned her into a goddess. "Do what?"

Penny gave her a look. "You're frowning, which means you're thinking, which means you are worrying. Don't do any of that."

"I'll try not to," Bree murmured with an apologetic smile.

"This is fantastic," Penny assured her. "Clint's sister-in-law and her team did an amazing job with the setup and decor, and the throwback pictures of Northbrook are incredible! It's a great touch."

"Thanks." Bree bit her lip, looking around one more time, positive she would find some glaring fault in all of this before the guests arrived. Fifty tables in the dining room with eight chairs apiece, five hundred dollars a plate. Each table had been perfectly set, draped with white linen and a green satin square underneath the centerpieces for Northbrook's colors. They'd even gone so far as to have centerpieces featuring the Northbrook Elite mascot, the Sabercat. The chandeliers sparkled brilliantly, and the white-and-green accent lighting on the walls added an almost mystical touch. The bar was set, with a dozen tall tables set up around there, and the tribute gallery had been fidgeted with so many times she'd made herself walk away.

The hotel was an exquisite setting, and the décor somehow managed to be elegant and honorific at this same time.

For an elite hockey club, of all things.

"Stop it," Penny warned. "You'll offset your rockin' look entirely if you have that pucker there all night." She pointed a finger at Bree's forehead, even tapping it softly. "Come on, we have done everything we can, and now it is out of our hands. And by the way, I would *kill* to look that good in anything." She stepped back and gestured to Bree in disbelief.

An uncomfortable, embarrassed blush rose on every conceivable inch of Bree's skin, and she rubbed her bare arms, averting her gaze. "Thanks. Trista flew out and took me shopping. Made me get a makeover. I think it works."

Penny scoffed loudly, which was the only way she ever did. "Uh, yeah!"

Bree smiled to herself and glanced down at her dress. It

really was a gorgeous gown, and she would never have purchased anything so expensive on her own. But Trista insisted, and Trista bought it, and there was nothing Bree could do about it.

She was secretly glad of it.

The berry-colored gown was sleek and formfitting without being shocking, and the skirts flowed from the bottom of her hips to the floor. Black-lace overlay covered the entirety, including a sheer section from neckline to bodice, with small clumps of beaded black flowers scattered throughout. It was sleeveless, and the sheerness extended around and down to her mid-back. The skirts swished just a little when she moved, and the entire ensemble was shockingly comfortable, which was a bonus to the overall appearance of it.

Trista had had her glam squad give Bree a loose, asymmetrical chignon with the occasional curled tendril hanging down, which left her feeling like the whole thing would come undone in a moment. She had been repeatedly assured that it would not, but she wasn't so sure. Add to all of that her makeup, which had blessedly been relatively neutral, aside from a smoky eyeshadow look, and Bree barely felt like herself.

In a good way.

If that was a thing.

Bree exhaled slowly and managed a smile at Penny. "Ready to be surrounded by former, current, and future hockey players?"

Her roommate flashed a quick grin. "I was born for this moment. I'm just going to go get Amy before she fusses over the family-fun section any further, okay?"

"Sounds good." Bree nodded and waved her on before turning to the nearest table and running her hand over the linen. Part of her wanted to stand at the entrance to the room and welcome people as they came in, but that was what the hotel staff was for. She wasn't supposed to micromanage the evening, as everything and everyone was in place to ensure the event ran smoothly.

Now if only she could breathe.

She shook her head, moving over to the bar, fighting the urge to get herself a drink before the event started.

Nobody would need that.

"Wow..."

Bree looked up, her smile spreading before her eyes took in the gorgeous sight of Clint McCarthy in a well-fitted tux. His blue eyes were wide as they slowly ran the length of her up and down, raising another blush on her skin. She smiled to herself at his not-quite-clean-shaven appearance and wondered, faintly, how many women would fan themselves over his picture when the photos from the event went out.

But he was *hers*.

And that made her smile further still.

"You're not so bad yourself," she informed him as she saw his corded throat working.

He met her gaze then, a small smile appearing. "I'm no match for you, and that's the truth." He came over to her, put a hand at her upper arm, and pressed a tender kiss to her brow. "I can't feel my knees, Bree," he whispered against her skin. "That's how beautiful you are."

She shivered, then pressed a quick kiss to his jaw, relieved when her lip color left no trace there. "Sorry not sorry," she whispered back.

Clint chuckled and held her close for a minute. She could feel the slight tremors in him, and she hugged herself closer because of it. He pulled back and stooped a little to meet her gaze squarely. "You ready for this?"

Bree gave him a shaky nod and an even shakier smile. "I think so. How are things outside?"

"Great. There's already lots of press, which makes curious people come over, and if I had my way, you and I would go back outside together and do a proper red-carpet entrance."

"No way," Bree said, shaking her head. "I'll pose with you for a few in here if I have to, but not out there."

"I'll take it." He winked, then turned to look behind them as some chatter met their ears. "Okay, showtime, babe. I promise not to hover, but I'll be close by if you need a rescue or an escape. Say the word, and we'll blow this joint for some burgers and shakes."

Bree laughed and put a hand to his face, her heart swelling within her. "I love you."

He kissed her quickly, humming with pleasure against her lips. "I love you too, sweetheart. Knock 'em dead." He gave her an encouraging nod, which she managed to return before he walked further into the event space.

He had a role to play tonight, as did she, and only time would tell if either of them succeeded.

A group of three men in equally fine tuxes approached her now, and she smiled at them at once.

"Well, hello there," the tallest one said. "Nice to see you off-screen."

"You too, Declan," she laughed, flushing just a little as he kissed her cheek in greeting.

"This is amazing, Bree," Rocco said with a grin, showing up Declan by giving her a kiss on both cheeks like the Italian he was. "Seriously awesome."

"Thank you. There was a lot of help."

Trane grunted softly, shaking his head with a smile. "Fido told us you'd push off the credit."

Bree gave him a disgruntled look. "You think I could do all this myself?"

"Yes," all three said in unison.

She rolled her eyes, smiling. "Whatever. Have you seen your video yet?"

They hadn't, and all brightened at the prospect of seeing it now, so she pointed them over to the Northbrook gallery, where all of that was set up. The video would go out to the news outlets the next day, and it was already slated for specials on all of the major news outlets.

It was beyond anything Bree had hoped for. There was no telling what kind of support would come from that kind of exposure, and the prospect was a thrilling one to contemplate.

Other guests began to trickle in, directed this way and that by the hotel staff depending on their interest. People of status and reputation in Chicago, former Northbrook players, and even some hockey legends came through, enjoying the food and the reminiscence of Northbrook in its glory days. Someone had even found footage of one of the greatest hockey games in Northbrook history and had it playing on several TV screens to one side.

Families began to arrive as well, and the children were wide-eyed at the opportunity to interact with their hockey heroes, to pose with them in the photo section, to try on full-sized hockey equipment, and to get some of the donated hockey paraphernalia from professional teams. The older guests were focused on the silent auction and the old photos, but they enjoyed mingling with each other and with the hockey players.

There were people everywhere, and Bree couldn't stop smiling at the sight of them. If all of these people donated to the fundraiser, some significant progress could be made to restoring Northbrook to its new future.

And there was no telling what it could do for Bree's future as well.

"Bree?"

She turned from her current position, still standing at one of the tall tables by the bar, which happened to have a good view of the entire place.

A tall, broad-shouldered man in a tux, brown hair with highlights pulled back into a clean man bun, smiled almost hesitantly at her as he approached. At his side was a little girl with the same dark hair and the same dark eyes, wearing a plum-colored dress with lace sleeves, a sparkling shoe on each foot.

"You came!" Bree exclaimed, keeping her focus on the little girl and bending as close to her level as her dress would allow. "Do you remember me, Hope?"

Hope smiled shyly and nodded, her hand clutching her father's tightly. "Yes, Miss Bree. Thank you for inviting me."

Bree looked up at Zane in surprise, and he grinned proudly, shrugging a shoulder. "Well, you are most welcome," Bree assured the little girl, returning her attention to her. "We ladies have to stick together tonight, right?"

"Right!" Hope looked at Bree's gown, her eyes going wide. "Your dress is so pretty, Miss Bree!"

Bree laughed, charmed by the hint of a Southern accent she heard in the young voice. "Thank you! I think your dress is so pretty, too. And your hair!" Bree shook her head with a sigh. "I tried so many times to get my hair that beautiful when I was your age. It never, ever worked."

Hope smiled up at her dad. "Daddy took me to a grown-up hair salon. He said I got to be fancy tonight."

Zane chuckled, shaking the hand holding his daughter's gently. "And then we went out to dinner, and now we're here!" He looked at Bree, still smiling. "I hope you don't mind that we're a bit late. I didn't want her to get caught up in the press fuss, so we snuck in the side."

Bree rose from Hope's level, nodding immediately. "Absolutely, I completely understand."

"I'm happy to go back out and do a formal entrance," he told her in all seriousness. "If this had been any other event, I probably would make a lot of noise about being here."

"Well, I would hate to cramp your usual style," Bree quipped in response. She smiled down at Hope and winked. "Hope can stay with me if you feel like doing that." She raised her eyes back to Zane's quickly. "But please, don't feel like you have to."

Zane shrugged and looked down at his daughter. "What do you think, baby girl? You wanna hang out with Miss Bree while Daddy puts on a show?"

Hope giggled and nodded, looking up at Bree. "Daddy *loves* putting on a show."

Bree and Zane laughed together, and another voice joined in with them.

They turned to see Jax just behind them, grinning broadly through his beard. "Very, very true, Miss Hope."

Hope still smiled but looked a little uncertain. "Daddy, is that one of the uncles?"

"Sure am," Jax said before her father could reply. "Uncle Jax at your service. And I am looking for a date tonight. Do you know where I could find a beautiful lady to come with me to the party? My family couldn't come tonight, so I am all by myself." He stuck out his lower lip in a pout for effect.

"I'll go with you, Uncle Jax!" Hope released her father's hand without hesitation and gripped Jax's, turning to Zane with a wave. "Bye, Daddy. Have fun with your show."

Jax snorted a laugh and lifted a brow as he and Hope moved away from them.

Zane sighed, shaking his head. "No going back now. She'll have them all wrapped around her finger in fifteen minutes."

"She's darling, Zane," Bree said quietly, taking in the man in a whole new light.

His smile turned very soft, his eyes still on his retreating daughter. "She is the better part of me. The best thing in my life." He glanced at Bree, his smile curving crookedly. "Who'd have thought, huh?"

She laughed, one arm wrapping around her midsection. "First impressions, maybe not, but I buy it now."

"Good. And thanks for doing this, Bree. Really." He squeezed her arm gently.

Bree nodded, strangely not at all embarrassed now. "My pleasure. Really."

Zane gave her cheek a quick kiss, then strode forward, tugging at his sleeves before sneaking out of a side door and disappearing from the event space.

Who'd have thought, he had asked.

Not Bree Stone, that's for sure.

Bree exhaled and looked around, surveying the area in an attempt to figure out where to go next. Her eyes landed on Clint, who had been watching her, and he smiled warmly.

She smiled back, blowing him a quick kiss.

He surprised her by excusing himself from the group he had been socializing with and coming over to her.

"You didn't have to leave them," she protested when he reached her. "I'm fine."

"I know. I just wanted to kiss you." He grinned and leaned in for a soft, tender kiss that could have gone on for ages but only lasted a moment.

Bree smiled in satisfaction, taking Clint's hand and bringing it to her lips.

"Okay, do you have to?"

Bree whirled with a wild grin at hearing that particular voice, and she dashed to her brother's waiting arms without hesitation. "Ryker!"

He chuckled and swept her up in a tight hug, then set her back down, brushing at her gown. "Sorry, sorry, don't want to smush your gown."

"Oh, like I care," Bree scoffed with a dismissive wave.

"My wife would care," Ryker pointed out. "And she scares me more than you."

Bree looked past him, frowning slightly. "Where *is* your wife?"

"Giving the photographers what they want. Pictures without me in them." He shook his head and shrugged. "Some of her actor friends are here, too, and most of her co-stars from the show, so it might be a minute."

Bree gaped at her brother, barely able to breathe. "Actors?" she finally asked. "I didn't . . . She didn't . . ."

Ryker laughed and tapped her chin to close her mouth. "There is a surprising number of hockey fans in Hollywood, Bree." He looked beyond Bree to Clint, and his smile shrank a little, but not entirely. "Clint."

Oh boy.

Bree grimaced and backed up, reaching for Clint's hand, which he immediately gave her. "Ryker, be nice."

"All I said was his name," her brother protested.

"And dropped the temperature in the room by twenty degrees," she shot back. "I love him, Ryker, and that's not going away."

Clint squeezed her hand tightly, and she found so much strength and comfort in that pressure, her throat tightened in response.

Ryker sighed and slid his hands into the pockets of his

tux pants. "I know. Trista gave me a lecture about the whole thing. And it's not like I can argue that he isn't a good guy. If you *had* to fall in love with anyone, I guess he'll do." He smiled at Clint genuinely and held out a hand. "I don't have to threaten you, right?"

Clint released Bree's hand to shake Ryker's. "Nope. I am well aware of what's at stake and what Bree is worth. I know full well she is out of my league."

"Please," Bree replied with a dry snort.

"Hush, sis, and let the wise man say his piece," Ryker scolded. He nodded at Clint, seeming satisfied. "All right, then. Feel like showing me around, Clint? I want to hear all about this club we're saving."

Clint agreed and, after giving Bree a quick kiss that made her blush, took her brother into the rest of the exhibit.

"Holy crap," Bree muttered to herself, exhaling slowly. That had gone better than she could have hoped, no matter how terrifying it had started out.

"Yeah, that went great!"

Bree looked over at her sister-in-law, now approaching in a formfitting gown of pure white, her hair elegantly swept back, looking like the incomparable movie star she was. "You said you were alone when I told you all that."

Trista smiled at her. "I was, at the start."

"You said you wouldn't tell him about . . ."

"I didn't tell him that part. He stepped out of the hotel room and had a minor panic attack, so he missed it." Trista rolled her eyes, still smiling. "Poor guy."

Bree's brow furrowed as she pictured the scenario. "But why didn't he call me back and yell at me or freak out? He totally would have."

Trista's smile turned mischievous. "I hid his phone and

distracted him appropriately. Then we had a logical discussion when he was reasonable again."

"That sounds disturbing," Bree replied.

"You're welcome." Trista turned slightly and waved. "Oh, and I think you'll want to see these two."

Bree looked around Trista, and her eyes immediately filled with tears, her feet moving at once. "Mom! Dad!"

Her parents hugged her as one, squeezing tight and both kissing the side of her head. "Hi, honey," her mom said, hugging her again without her dad involved. "We are so proud of you for pulling this off! For all of your hard work and what you are doing . . . so proud."

Bree blinked back a sheen of tears, pulling back and taking her mom's hand. "What are you guys doing here? It's a long trip from Baltimore, and I'd understand . . . "

"Do you think we would miss this?" her father interrupted gently. "We love Clint, and we want to do everything we can to save his hockey club. And you had to know we wanted to support you."

"And we are so happy the two of you are together," her mom added with a bright smile. "Aubrey and I have been talking, and we were thinking . . . "

"We should join Clint and Ryker in a tour," Trista overrode in a firm tone. "Let's catch up before they get too far." She winked at Bree as she ushered them along. "We'll be back in a bit."

Bree waved, mouthing a quick thank-you to Trista, then put her chilled hands to her overheated cheeks. Between the excitement of the night and her family, she'd probably be red in the face for the entire night, if not beyond.

"There's who I've been looking for!"

Unsure she could take one more surprise, Bree glanced to her right in trepidation only to grin with relief. "Hi, Grizz."

Sporting his iconic beard, Grizz came over to her and gave her a big hug. "Hi, kiddo." He pulled back to look her over, nodding in approval. "You look fantastic. How would you like to date my brother?"

"Sounds like a plan." She shared a teasing grin with him and released a heavy breath. "Oh my gosh, Grizz, I'm exhausted."

He chuckled and leaned his elbows on the table next to her. "I bet! You've been running yourself ragged. If I were you, I'd sneak away before the thing is over and go back to my hotel."

"Don't tempt me." She looked around him, frowning. "Where's your wife?"

Grizz shrugged and gestured to the room as a whole. "Somewhere. She's so excited to be here, it's not even funny. Wouldn't surprise me if she starts taking hockey lessons pretty soon. Well, after the baby comes."

Bree had been nodding in amusement, but the words jerked her out of the repetitive motion, and she slapped Grizz's arm. "Baby? Grizz!" She gave him another tight hug, squealing in excitement. "Oh my gosh, congratulations!"

"Thank you," he laughed, hugging her back. "Rachel's incredible, hasn't been more than mildly queasy for three months. She's going to have to stop dancing soon, which has her cranky, but . . . " He trailed off, smiling. "I should have her take my place playing against Clint on the ice."

"On the what?" Bree snickered at the thought, shaking her head. "You can't play Clint on the ice."

"I can too," he shot back, pretending at an offended air. "Who do you think taught the boy to play?"

Bree gave him a dubious look. "You can't do anything that might injure you for next season. I know the rules."

Grizz raised a brow. "Who says I can't play a one-on-one

game against my kid brother? Especially if we're raising money on it."

"Money?" Bree repeated, all playing gone. "What money?"

Again, Grizz gestured to the room. "What do you think?"

"No..."

"Yes." Grizz nodded very firmly three times. "It's all arranged. Tomorrow morning, Clint and I play a little one-on-one and raise some money, all of which goes to your Northbrook fundraising. Well, in addition to what the Flames and I are already donating."

Bree put a hand over Grizz's arm, gripping tight. "Grizz, I can't ask you to do that."

"You didn't," he told her easily. "Clint did."

All of the air vanished from Bree's lungs. "What?"

Grizz nodded. "Yep. Called the entire Six Pack individually, got each of us to spread the word, and because of that, pretty soon you'll see the social media challenge start trending."

"The what?"

He grinned slowly, raising a dark brow. "He didn't tell you?"

"I mean, we joked about it..." Bree stammered.

"Ha. Jokes. This is no joke, Bree." Grizz looked over his shoulder, then leaned closer to her, lowering his voice. "His team is doing double duty, raising money for Northbrook and the local St. Louis team."

Bree's mouth moved silently, no words forming.

Grizz took pity on her. "Teams everywhere are coming out to support their local organizations, Bree. Some of them are even adding to the Northbrook fund. It's caught fire. Look up #savenorthbrook and #mashupchallenge."

"I don't have my phone," she said weakly.

FACEOFF

He pulled his out and scrolled for a second to find a video, then set the phone down on the table for her to watch.

Clint stood on a basketball court, of all things, and gave a short speech about what they were doing and why, then challenged Jax's team, the Chicago Flyers, to do the next challenge.

Suddenly a good portion of Clint's teammates were running up and down the court, dribbling and shooting the basketball and playing against other guys she didn't recognize.

"Those are the St. Louis Daredevils. The pro baseball team."

Bree smiled and glanced up at Grizz. "Hockey and baseball guys playing basketball?"

Grizz returned her smile. "Those are the rules. No team can play the sport they do professionally. It would be an unfair advantage."

"Of course." Bree shook her head and continued watching the video. "This is amazing."

"What's amazing is how I creamed Jax in Ping-Pong," Grizz boasted gruffly as the game on his phone morphed into a ridiculous exhibition of a slam dunk contest.

Bree sniffed back tears and grinned at him through watery eyes. "I'd like to see that."

Grizz smiled and winked, pocketing his phone. "You started this, Bree. This whole event is incredible, but you know what's even better? It's going to keep going. It's going to get huge. I don't know if I should tell you this, but my general manager asked me about this and is looking into local baseball programs to support. You may want to put a name on this puppy and get incorporated, because your phone is going to start ringing."

"Are you serious?" she whispered, her hands flying to her mouth.

"Yep." He threw an arm around her shoulder and pulled her in, giving her head a quick kiss. "Welcome to the family, sis. If I know my brother, he's not letting you go. And I'd have to kill him if he did."

Bree giggled and peered up at this giant of a baseball player, this icon in his sport, who had only ever been Grizz to her. "If he lets me go, he better take me with him."

Grizz barked a laugh and steered Bree away from her safe table, wandering with her through the crowded, noisy, beautiful event. "Come on, kiddo. Let's see what you've done, and what kind of damage we can do."

She slipped her arm around his waist and let him stroll with her, her chest tightening and releasing in an almost steady pattern as she looked, really looked, at the place.

It had come together. It had really turned into everything she had hoped for. If nothing else came from all of this, at least tonight had panned out.

She caught sight of Clint across the room, chatting and laughing with her family, with his family, and with Declan and Rocco, who now had a grinning Hope between them, her hands in theirs. Clint saw Bree and gave her a warm and tender smile, even from that distance causing her to silently sigh.

She put her hand over her heart and patted twice, then pointed at him, mouthing the words, "I love you."

Clint's smile grew, and his hand came to his heart and thumped twice, then blew a kiss to her.

They stared at each other, smiling, for as long as Bree could see him, not bothering to redirect Grizz in that direction.

There would be time for telling Clint just how much he meant to her; how much his actions had meant to her. How she couldn't have done any of this without him.

How she wouldn't want to.

"Hey, Grizz," Bree said through the lump forming in her throat, "how would you feel about a beard showdown between you and Jax tonight?"

"Oh ho ho," Grizz rumbled with a laughable superiority. "Bring it on."

EIGHTEEN

"AND WE JUST want to thank whoever put on the event for giving my daughters the opportunity to meet such great hockey players who encouraged them to follow their dreams and become great hockey players themselves. What a classy night. We will support Northbrook forever!"

Bree smiled and snuggled herself further into the corner of Clint's couch, the warmth of hearing such a post centering in her chest and spreading out to the tips of each finger.

She'd read all of them already, but hearing Clint read them out loud made them seem more real.

Not even a week out from the gala, and their momentum hadn't slowed at all. The internet had exploded with coverage and posts, volunteers had cleaned up the landscaping of the Northbrook facility and planned on planting several things in the spring, and the interview video of Clint and The Pit had been replayed so many times they were all sick of it.

Sort of.

Clint's social media campaign had become even more popular than Grizz had predicted; dozens of videos popped up every day from different teams of all levels. Even non-athletic groups were joining in. Only this morning she had seen a video of a police department having a water fight with the fire department, both groups pledging money to Northbrook. Rachel McCarthy's dance company had changed the game by challenging other dance companies to do improv dance in Halloween costumes, which was trending now among dance companies across the country. One of the New York football teams had challenged their basketball team to a synchronized swimming competition, which already had over a million views, and a new round of more ridiculous challenges were popping up in response.

All of them used the Northbrook hashtag, and each one produced a donation of some size to their project.

What was even better than all of this, if that was possible, was that the numbers had come in, and they had raised enough money to get Northbrook out of its current trouble and start in on a better financial foundation. It was a long way from saving the club indefinitely, everyone knew, but it gave them time to get things right.

It was a start. It was a really good start.

Clint chuckled, his arm draped comfortably around her bent knees, and he patted her leg, shaking his head. "Bree, these posts go on and on. Forget saving Northbrook; you changed people's lives."

"Stop that," she murmured, smiling with embarrassment, burying her face into the couch.

"Nope, you're just going to have to listen to all of this praise like a good philanthropist," he insisted without concern, his fingers tracing absent patterns on her jeans. "Modesty is all well and good, babe, but when you are exceptional..."

"Clint," Bree begged, her voice muffled through the cushions.

He laughed softly. "Fine, I'll stop. Come out."

She exhaled and turned her face to give him a suspicious look. "You'll stop?"

"Yes," he told her with a serious look, though there was mischief lingering in his expression.

She narrowed her eyes but sat up and leaned closer to him, resting her arm on top of his. "You're going to have to take some credit too, you know."

He quirked his brows at her, not at all concerned by that. "Am I? Whatever for?"

"Oh, I don't know." She made a face, gesturing helplessly. "Maybe a viral social media campaign that is *still* picking up momentum. Something that actually crossed the boundaries of sport and community and has elementary school kids taking up donations for Northbrook."

Clint's pleased smile was intense but brief as he sobered. "Technically, the campaign is all Penny's work. She's the one who got it all set up."

Bree shook her head from side to side. "Huh-uh. Penny is a genius, and she knows social media and advertising like nobody else, but this is you, babe. You are the one who made the calls and got the involvement from athletes who make an impact. You'll never know how much it means to me."

"You are the one saving my old hockey club, Bree." He smiled at her and rubbed her leg gently. "The score is always going to have you ahead here."

They'd been over this again and again since the gala, and they had never made any progress. He insisted all the credit was hers, she insisted he deserved more, and their extremes were only going to get more and more ridiculous.

Bree leaned her head on their arms, smiling at Clint in adoration, saying nothing.

He returned her smile with one of his own. "What?"

She shrugged, lacing their fingers together. "I'm just happy. That's all."

"Good." His smile crinkled his eyes briefly. "You should be. It was incredible, Bree. You should hear what the guys have been saying, not to mention the Six Pack, and my team is so mad they couldn't all come..."

Bree giggled softly and brought his hand to her lips. "I didn't mean the gala. Yes, I'm happy the gala went well, and yes, I'm happy that we have enough money now to really get going with saving the club, but none of that is what I meant."

"No?"

She shook her head. "I'm happy with *you*. Happier than I thought I could be, happier than I've ever been." She smiled further, holding his hand close to her. "This is it, isn't it? What everyone writes songs and poems and stories about?"

Clint nodded slowly, reaching out with his free hand to push a lock of hair behind her ear and stroke her cheek. "Yeah, it is. I don't write songs or poems or stories; I'm just a dumb hockey player..."

"Stop." She rolled her eyes and heaved a mock irritated sigh.

"But," he went on, "if that doesn't bother you too much, I'll happily rub your feet every night just to show you how much I love you."

Bree snickered at the image. "I'll take you up on that, but I won't need it every night."

"Good," Clint said with a heaving breath of relief. "My hands are not strong enough to do every night, but it was the only noble thing I could think of."

"My hero," she replied dryly. She bit her lip and looked down at their joined hands, reluctance and hesitation seeping into her happy moment.

She had to tell him; arrangements had to be made soon, and before they knew it, the semester would be over.

What would he say? How would they do this?

How *could* she do this?

"You're thinking a million miles a minute, and I can smell the smoke from the gears."

Bree looked up at him with another smile, her fingers stroking against his. "I have to tell you something."

"I thought you might."

She exhaled slowly, keeping her eyes trained on his. "I heard from my advisor today. The graduate committee made their decision on my internship."

Clint's eyes widened. "And?"

Bree swallowed, hesitating. "They've accepted my proposal. I can start my own nonprofit for my internship, provided they get regular reports on my progress. There will be no claims to the business itself from their end, no liability to them, no ownership by the school."

"Bree!" Clint exclaimed, his free hand flying to cup her cheek once more. "Baby, that's fantastic! Congratulations, you deserve this!"

"Thank you, I'm so relieved." She let her smile widen, then fade. "There is one more stipulation they had, though."

"Sure, understandable, since you need the credit for school."

Bree bit her lip. "Clint . . . "

He sobered at once, his thumb brushing over her cheek softly. "Tell me."

Her eyes began to burn. "Since Northbrook is my test client, so to speak, they insist that I need to be on-site, just as anyone else doing an internship would have to be. In Chicago."

Clint froze, his mouth forming an O shape as the thought settled on him and started processing.

Bree waited without speaking, rubbing his hand over and over, not sure if she was soothing him or herself with the action.

Maybe both of them.

"Okay," Clint said slowly, beginning to nod. "Okay. That makes sense. You'd have to go somewhere for an internship, right? Probably wouldn't be lucky enough to find a local one."

"Probably not," Bree agreed.

He nodded again. "When would you need to be there?"

"Shortly after next semester starts," Bree murmured, a hitch in her voice. "If not before. I'll be there until at least the beginning of May. Come back here maybe once a month if my committee wants to meet."

"Maybe once a month," he repeated.

Bree's eyes watered now, the reality of the situation hitting her with a sharp pain. "Yeah."

"Okay." Clint's eyes narrowed as he stared at her, his thumb stroking her cheek once more. "I need to do something, okay?"

"Okay."

He pulled out his phone, scrolled quickly, then hit a button and set the phone down on the table, the ringing audible on the speakerphone.

"Hi, honey!" the voice of Clint's mother called, cheery in tone and bright in aspect. "You would not believe how many calls I've been getting after that gala. I hope you and Bree have a plan for this—"

"Mom, you're on speaker," Clint told her, cutting off whatever else she was going to say. "Bree's here too."

"Oh! Hi, sweetie!"

Bree smiled at the phone. "Hi, Mrs. McCarthy."

"Aubrey. I insist."

Bree's cheeks flushed. "Hi, Aubrey."

"Mom, I have a question," Clint said, stroking Bree's leg soothingly.

"I might have an answer."

Bree gave Clint a questioning look, but he only smiled.

"Can Bree stay in the guest room at the house?" he asked, his eyes on Bree.

"Clint!" Bree hissed, shaking her head.

Aubrey hesitated on the phone. "Of course, why would you even need to ask?"

Clint grinned broadly. "She'll need it for about four months starting in January."

There was a beat, and then Aubrey squealed, the sound garbling slightly through the speaker. "Oh my gosh, yes! Yes, yes, of course! Bree, you're moving to Chicago?"

Bree bit back a snarky remark to her boyfriend and forced a smile. "Yeah, I am. My advisor approved my using Northbrook as my internship, and she wants me in Chicago to work on it."

"Oh, sweetie, you *have* to stay with us. Chicago can be so expensive. It would be so much cheaper to stay with us. No pressure, of course; you won't offend me if you want an apartment. Our guest room is huge, and it has its own bathroom attached, so you would have all the privacy you'd want. It's all in the basement with an open den, so you'd really have the entire floor to yourself. Private entrance, if you'd want it. You don't have to answer now, but we would love it if you'd stay with us."

There was something very sweet about the obviously excited, if rushed, offer, and Bree warmed at the thought of living with a family while not feeling like a child. She could save money and have access to everything she would need to work on the Northbrook project. And to be with Clint's family...

She would still be connected to him even while they were apart.

A lump formed in her throat as she stared at him. How had he known she would love the idea the moment she heard it? How had he known she would need this?

"That sounds great, Aubrey," Bree managed thickly, pulling Clint's hand close to her again, as she couldn't possibly kiss him senseless while on the phone with his mother. "I think I would love that."

"Yay!" Aubrey cheered. "Oh, that would be so fun. I promise not to smother you or be nosy or anything like that. You just come and go as you please and join us for dinner whenever you feel like it. Bree! I've never had a girl live in my house with me. You can't imagine how happy this makes me! I'm already thinking of things we can do, and—"

"Okay, Mom, we gotta go," Clint said with a laugh. "You guys still okay to come down next weekend for the game?"

Aubrey laughed herself. "Clint, are you telling me to shut up and leave Bree alone?"

"More or less."

"I'm gonna have to hurt you, son . . ."

Bree snickered at the threat, though she could hear Aubrey's warm smile in it.

"I'll trap you in a bear hug, Mama," Clint shot back.

They heard Aubrey sigh in resignation. "Yes, honey, we're coming next weekend, and we'd love to take you and Bree out after the game. Plan on us, okay?"

"Sure will. Love you."

"Love you too. Love you *both*. Bye now."

Bree was speechless as the call ended, staring at the phone on the coffee table in amazement.

She'd just said . . .

But how . . . ?

Clint picked up the phone and dialed another number while Bree struggled through her emotions, entirely without words.

"Hey, Clint," Rachel's voice said cheerily. "What's up? You miss me already?"

"Sure do," he replied. "Bree's here, and she's got something to tell you."

Bree glared at Clint through her tear-filled eyes, but he only smiled and inclined his head towards the phone.

Clearing her throat, Bree shook her head and said, "Hey, Rach . . . I'm, uh . . . I'm moving to Chicago next semester. You feel like being my guide around the city?"

Rachel cheered loudly, making Clint and Bree laugh together. "Another Six Pack Sib in my neighborhood? Heck yeah! I got you, girl!"

"You're a Six Pack spouse, Rach," Bree reminded her, not that the status negated the sibling role, but it was worth stating.

"Sisters before misters, Bree."

Bree coughed a laugh. "Don't tell Grizz."

"He's right here. Glaring."

"Sounds like him," Clint muttered good-naturedly.

"Does this mean you'll come visit us more, Clint?" Rachel demanded.

Clint's gaze returned to Bree, his smile softening. "I'll be visiting Bree every chance I can. You guys can tag along sometimes."

Grizz's rumbling laughter could be heard, and Rachel snickered. "Fair enough. See you soon, okay?"

"Bye," Clint and Bree said together before Clint hung up.

Silence filled the room as they stared at each other.

"Why'd you do that?" Bree asked with genuine curiosity.

Clint turned more towards her, bringing both arms around her knees and taking her hands, cupping them together and rubbing his thumbs over the tops. "I need you to be taken care of while you're living in Chicago. You don't need anyone watching out for you or protecting you or anything like that, but I want you to be surrounded by people who love you. If I can't be there with you, at least now I can guarantee that."

"I'm a big girl, Clint," Bree told him gently. "I can handle it."

"I know that. Believe me, I am well aware how independent, impressive, and incredible you are." He pulled her hands over the tops of her knees, kissing them softly. "If I've overstepped, tell me. I just want you to know you're not alone whether you're here or there. You'll always have someone."

Bree pulled her hands free of his and placed them on either side of his face, leaning close. "I love you, Clint McCarthy."

He exhaled in relief, his eyes searching hers. "So you're okay with this?"

"With you taking care of me?" She pressed her lips to his gently, but with insistence. "Yes," she told him, breaking off. "I'm okay with that."

He grinned and pulled her forward until she was sitting in his lap. "Good. And you know, it's a short train ride up to Chicago. Just a few hours. I can work around my playing schedule."

Bree ran her fingers through his hair, tender affection filling her chest. "You can't go crazy, babe. You're in season."

"Who said I would go crazy? I just said I'd come up when I could."

"Oh, is that what you said?"

"That's what I said," he insisted, patting her back playfully. "And you can still go to plenty of hockey games to keep up your terminology and get your fix when you miss me. Jax can get you all the Flyers tickets you want."

Bree snorted softly. "With all the work I have to do? I only have time for your games."

Clint sighed and pulled her close, linking his hands behind her back. "I love you."

"Because I'm not going to Jax's games?" Bree laughed.

He nodded. "That, and so much more." He pressed her to him, giving her a long, slow, thorough kiss that made her body buzz.

Bree broke off and dusted a soft kiss high on Clint's cheek. "I will go to Grizz's games, though. No offense."

Clint hissed, pulling away from her playfully. "Still love you very much, but that smarts."

She shrugged. "I'm a baseball girl. Sorry."

He gave her a scolding look. "You're *my* girl, Bree Stone. Chicago doesn't change that."

"You're right," she admitted, feeling her lips pull into a smile she hoped would dazzle him. "I am your girl, no matter where either of us is, and my man plays hockey." She touched her brow to his, peering deeply into his piercing blue eyes. "Guess that makes me a hockey girl now."

"It had better," he growled before kissing her again.

And it was very, very convincing.

EPILOGUE

THE ROOM WAS filled to the brim with people, every table full and a few stragglers desperately looking for any seat anywhere.

Standing room only for an awards dinner.

He'd never have expected that, but it made everything better, in his mind.

Bree deserved as much attention as she could get.

She'd hate every minute of it.

Clint glanced over at her as she sat next to him, her attention on the plate before her and what remained of the dinner on it.

She was stunning this evening, and every glance at her hit that truth home once again. She'd chosen to wear white, the dress barely showing the tops of her shoulders, her thick brown hair curled and half pulled up. Her makeup was natural, which he always preferred, but Trista had convinced her to go with a little extra on the eye shadow in what they called a smoky eye.

He didn't get it, but he loved how it brought out the green in her hazel eyes, and he loved what that did to his chest and his knees.

He watched as she fiddled around with a piece of lettuce on her plate, her fork turning it this way and that without doing anything to bring it to her mouth.

The sight made him smile. Bree was nervous.

She didn't need to be; this wasn't the Oscars. She already knew she was getting this award.

One quick speech, and it would be done.

But Bree didn't like public speaking at things like this. She preferred a conference room full of eager board members willing to listen to and heed her advice, or encouraging a room full of kids to participate in physical activities while introducing them to local programs.

She really had a way with people, but being on display was one of her least favorite things.

It wasn't a problem when Clint was the target and she was on his arm, but when it was about her, it was a big deal.

He loved that about her.

She had always described herself as a background person. He thought she deserved the spotlight.

They were never going to agree on this.

Clint put a hand over Bree's where it rested in her lap. She looked at him at once, her lips pulling into a small smile. "Wanna run away?"

He laughed softly but shook his head. "And miss your big moment? I don't think so, sweetheart."

She wrinkled her nose briefly in disappointment, though he sensed she was playing. She looked over at the stage at the front of the room and exhaled roughly. "I just want them to get started. Get this over with. Then we can go home, and I can put on some sweats."

"I love the way you look in sweats."

Bree quirked her brows in his favorite teasing manner. "Something to look forward to, then."

"Ladies and gentlemen," the emcee intoned from the podium on the stage. "Ladies and gentlemen, we're going to proceed to the awards portion of the ceremony at this time. Don't worry, your dessert will be coming around shortly."

The room laughed, and Clint smiled, still holding Bree's hand tightly.

"To present the first award of the evening," the emcee went on, "please welcome hockey Hall of Famer Coach Hal Fenwick."

Clint grinned and looked at Bree, who'd had no idea of the identity of her presenter. She was gaping at the stage, too shocked to applaud.

Coach Fenwick approached the podium, making eye contact with Bree and Clint, waving at them both.

Clint raised two fingers and saluted, nodding his thanks.

Bree's hold on Clint's hand squeezed almost painfully tight now.

"Thank you," Coach Fenwick said to the crowd. "Thank you very much."

He looked down at the podium, then cleared his throat and raised his eyes. "There are some people who see the world as it is and have the drive to change it. To see a problem and suggest a solution. To find a cause in need of direction, take it up, and make it their banner. This is what Bree Stone and her team at Prime Outreach Incorporated have done. From their very first project with the Northbrook Elite Hockey Club, whose support videos are still some of the most viewed on the internet, they have set out to restore athletic clubs in trouble and to bring back the power of a team, a sport, an activity, and in some cases, an entire community."

Coach Fenwick paused, smiling directly at Bree, seeming to speak only to her now. "Looking back, it is impossible to think that it has been a mere eighteen months since their very first event, when you consider all that Prime has accomplished. All that Bree has accomplished. I first met her in person at that very first event, a fundraising gala in Chicago thrown together in a short time, specifically to raise money for a club that I had devoted most of my professional career to. A club that meant everything to me. Bree, at that time, barely knew the sport, according to various sources who shall remain nameless."

A rumble of laughter rippled across the room.

"That evening," he went on, "was a special one for me. I don't think Bree will even remember meeting me, considering there were so many guests having such a great time, and she managed the entire thing without breaking a sweat. But I knew I would remember her. I knew that she was something special. I knew that she would go on to do great things. And despite what she has accomplished, how she has impressed, the difference she has made, her career is only just beginning, and her work, and the work of the company she founded, will only get more and more impressive, making more of a difference than she, or the world, will ever know." His smile grew and he dipped his chin in a nod. "It is my privilege and honor to present this year's Rising Star award to Bree Stone and Prime Outreach Incorporated."

Applause filled the air, and Clint released a rough exhale, turning to look at Bree. Her eyes were fixed on the stage, her throat working twice on a swallow. Her eyes met his, her lips trembling as she tried to smile.

"I love you," Clint whispered.

"I love you too." She leaned forward for a quick kiss, then rose, smoothing her dress before moving to the stage.

Clint got to his feet and clapped, his chest and throat tightening almost painfully with pride. He heard some whistles and whoops from somewhere behind him, which made him smile. Clearly Bree had some fans in the room, which was only right.

Bree took her statuette from Coach Fenwick, giving him a tight hug and smiling when he kissed her cheek, whispering something in her ear. She nodded and moved to the podium, exhaling shakily, one hand pushing back a short lock of hair falling over her brow.

"Wow," she said with an almost breathless smile for the crowd. "Wow, thank you."

The applause settled, and they all took their seats.

Bree inhaled, exhaled, then shook her head. "I can't believe I am really here tonight. That I've done anything to deserve an award or attention or that Coach Fenwick would come out of retirement to hand out one more trophy to a kid."

Clint chuckled along with Coach and the rest of the room.

"I have been surrounded by sports my entire life," Bree admitted, turning serious. "My brother is a baseball player, and I'll let you guess who." She paused for another laugh. "I never minded going to his games. I can't say I always paid attention to them, but I went. I learned to love the sport that he loved. I saw the bond he had with his team in every level of his career. I saw the joy that it brought to his life and the dedication that he put into that sport to become great. The man he became because of that sport. And then I met a hockey player."

She paused again and looked over at Clint, her smile reappearing. "He changed my life. Because of him, I learned what a slash is, what boards are, and why in the world there are so many fistfights in a sport using blades to move on ice."

The room erupted with laughter, and Clint grinned in delight. She was so good up there, and were it not for the fact that he knew her so well, he would never have suspected that her knees were shaking beneath her skirts.

"I saw that same love," Bree went on. "That same dedication. That same passion and spirit, that feeling of a team becoming a family. When the situation of the Northbrook Elite Hockey Club became known to me, it was almost immediately obvious to me that this was what I wanted to do with my life. This was what I wanted to dedicate my career to. This was a difference that I could make."

She paused, then lifted her chin and looked out at the audience, a new strength and light filling her. "I am not an athlete myself, and I am the first to admit that I am far from it. This has never been about athletics. This has always been, and will always be, about passion, about heart, about community, and about healthy physical activity."

Clint caught how Bree's hand shook, not in fear, but with the passion she felt for her cause.

"It's about giving every kid the opportunity to be part of a team, to develop not only athletic skills but life skills. To prove that no one is defined by where they live, how much money they have, or who they know."

Applause interrupted Bree then, and she smiled as she waited for it to fade.

She swallowed hard and wet her lips. "Every club or program or team that POI supports, restores, or sponsors gives back to their community and brings their young athletes, dancers, performers, or students powerful experiences that can shape who they are and who they will become. *They* are changing lives, not us, and certainly not me. All we can do, and all we want to do, is make sure they are able to keep going, keep building, and continue to do just that. Thank you very much."

Every person in the room was on their feet, cheering for

this powerful woman and her impassioned speech, her call to each of them to join her without any hint of recruitment in her words.

That was the effect of Bree Stone.

The woman he loved.

Clint shook his head to himself, applauding with the rest of the room, smiling with all the love and pride in the world as she left the stage and came back to their table. He opened his arms, and she walked right into them, clinging to him while exhilarated tremors cascaded through her frame.

"Amazing," Clint murmured in her ear. "I am so proud of you."

She pulled back and smiled up at him, relief evident in every feature. "I couldn't do any of this without you, Clint. Not any of it."

He grinned and shook his head, helping her to her seat. "I find that very hard to believe, but thank you."

"It's true," she insisted as he sat, taking his hand. "You are everything to me. You have to know that."

"I am glad to hear you say so."

His heart pounded furiously in his chest, but there could be no more perfect moment than this.

"Now that you've taken the athletics world by storm," he murmured, reaching into the inside pocket of his suit coat, "maybe you'd like to take something else as well."

He put the small box on the table and slid it pointedly towards her.

Bree stared at the still-closed box, barely breathing. Her eyes lifted to Clint's, round and dark. "Clint McCarthy, are you serious right now?"

Clint smiled quickly and reached over to lift the lid of the box, eliciting a gasp from her. "I've only been more serious once in my life, and that was when I told you I love you."

One of Bree's hands covered her mouth for the space of several breaths, then went to her heart as she swallowed. "Oh my . . . it's so beautiful."

"Still doesn't hold a candle to you, love." Clint slid from his chair, going down to one knee before her, drawing the attention of the other guests around them now. "Bree Stone, will you marry me?"

Bree beamed at him with all the brightness and glory of the sun, frantically nodding. "Yes! Yes, yes, I would love to." She reached for him, and he rose, kissing her fiercely as one of his hands slid to the base of her neck, careful to avoid ruining her hair.

Whoops and applause lit the air around them, and they laughed into their kiss. Clint pulled back and tugged the ring from its box, sliding it onto her finger. "It should fit," he said unnecessarily as he pressed it to the base. "Trista gave me some very exact measurements."

"Trista knew?" Bree asked in delighted shock.

"A few people knew," he admitted as he pointed just behind her.

Bree whirled to see her entire family, his family, and most of their friends approaching from some of the outer tables, where they had been safely hidden from her view. She turned back to Clint, grinning even while tears began to trickle down her cheeks. "You sneak!"

He shrugged, laughing. "You always said you wanted your family there when you get engaged. You didn't think I was listening, but I took some very careful notes."

She closed the distance between them and threw her arms around his neck, drawing him down for a sound kiss. "I love you, Clint."

Clint wiped away one of her tears, thinking his heart

might actually explode within him. "I love you, Bree. Always will."

Bree kissed him again and winked with a hint of promise, then turned to face their family and friends, wiggling her newly ringed finger for all to see.

Rebecca Connolly writes romances, both period and contemporary, because she absolutely loves a good love story. She has been creating stories since childhood, and there are home videos to prove it! She started writing them down in elementary school and has never looked back. She currently lives in Indiana, spends every spare moment away from her day job absorbed in her writing, and is a hot cocoa addict.

www.ingramcontent.com/pod-product-compliance
Lightning Source LLC
LaVergne TN
LVHW021808060526
838201LV00058B/3287